CARRIE BEAMER

**Evernight Teen ®**

**www.evernightteen.com**

Copyright© 2020

ISBN: 978-0-3695-0174-5

Cover Artist: Jay Aheer

Editor: Melissa Hosack

## ALL RIGHTS RESERVED

# CARRIE BEAMER

# DEDICATION

For my son Justin, without you this story would have never come to fruition. Thanks for the journey.

For my son Peyton, who somehow managed to eat the meals I slopped together on all those nights when his dinner took a backseat to my revisions. Thanks for the patience.

For Megan Tripp, even in your hardest hours you found time to be my cheerleader. You're the best. What a year!

For Paige McClellan, you have believed in me for over 25 years, and I couldn't be more grateful for your sisterhood.

# ACKNOWLEDGEMENTS

I never would have finished this book without the encouragement of my family and friends. Thank you all for believing in me.

Thank you to Leslie Hahner and Maura Jortner for showing me the ropes into this crazy journey of publication. Thank you to Michael Mario Albrecht for helping me clean this manuscript up in its earliest stages. I learned more from you than I want to admit.

# CARRIE BEAMER

I am very grateful to Sarah Barkoff Palma. This book moved forward because of your insight and for giving me the confidence to keep writing. Thank you for all of it.

Finally, thank you to Stuart White. This book would not be possible without you. You're changing the lives of writers all over the world. WriteMentor changed mine!

Carrie Beamer

Copyright © 2020

## Chapter One

Anything worth talking about in my mediocre existence always starts with Tessa. Always has.

Glancing up as I walk in, Tessa stands in her bra and underwear, with one leg balancing on top of the bathroom sink, shaving her long leg. The top of her short, strawberry blonde hair, recently cut into a Molly Ringwald bob, is pulled back with a pink butterfly clip. She, and every other girl in the country, copied the look as soon as they left the movie theater after seeing *Sixteen Candles* last year. Everyone except me. I favor Kelly LeBrock's look from *Weird Science*. Tessa says I have the boobs to pull it off. But I think it all comes down to the hair—I've got the same crazy tangle of curly brown hair that's so voluminous that it kind of looks like I stuck my finger into an electrical outlet. But in a good way.

"If you didn't shave, you totally better because there's going to be some seriously cute guys at Lori's house tonight." Tessa's mouth curls into a sly smirk of rebellion.

"Ugh, but I hate shaving my legs unless I'm in the shower," I say, bending over to run my hands down my shins and doing a stubble check.

"So, like, dry shave." She shrugs and turns her attention back to her legs. "You'll thank me later." Tessa finishes up and hands me the razor.

"What exactly is it that we're doing tonight?" I avoid looking at the razor that's so full of Tessa's leg hairs that I want to gag.

"No questions remember? I promised you an exciting Saturday night, and I'm totally going to deliver. I'm stoked for the surprise I've got coming your way." She lets out a nasally squeal of happiness.

"What have you done now?" I slap my hand over my mouth, realizing I asked another question. The familiar feeling of being terrified that Tessa's going to get us in over our heads takes hold. It's like the mix of thrill and dread you feel when locking in your seatbelt on a roller coaster. You have no clue how the ride's going to go, but you want to do it anyway.

Since Tessa moved to a new school last year, she met a new group of friends that I don't know—thanks to being stuck at home babysitting my brother almost every night of the week when my dad's working overtime. Gathering from what she's told me, some of them are a bit out of control, and that's saying something coming from me. My favorite pastime is sneaking a smoke while stealing a couple sips of my dad's beer when he's passed out on the couch after pulling an all-nighter at work. The last time Tessa was at her new friend Lori's house, she took two shots of tequila and went skinny-dipping in a pond—with Lori's mother.

"Let's just say you need a change, and me being the awesome best friend that I am recognizes that this change needs to come in the form of a really cute boy." She grins and slaps me on my butt. My skin stings a little in her wake. "Also, I can't wait for you to meet Riley. I know I don't have the best track record for picking a decent guy, but he's a total keeper."

"I think I'll be the judge of that. You thought Brett Harrington was a keeper, and he was more of a throw him back loser," I say, concentrating on running the razor up my leg in a smooth shave.

Tessa having a surprise for me that involves her new crowd is what's making me so skeptical about tonight. She's getting involved in things we've never done before. I guess she tried smoking pot about a month ago at Lori's house but said it was no big deal. She explained that she coughed so much she felt like an idiot and hasn't tried it again.

It made me sort of jealous because I always thought that if Tessa and I ever did try pot, it would be together. Realizing that's a stupid thing to get jealous about, I push it from my mind. It's not like she's replacing me. You can't replace your best friend from second grade who trusted you enough to let you teach her how to use a tampon at age thirteen. It was a bonding experience I could've done without, but I couldn't continue to let her wear a pillow between her legs every month.

Unhooking her bra, Tessa takes it off and stands in front of the mirror, doing what I call her are-my-boob's-bigger-routine. It looks like she's doing some weird mating ritual with her arms, flying up and back, her naked chest out for all to see. She's done this since the fifth grade, and it never ceases to amaze me that she hasn't caught onto the fact that it's a waste of time. But that doesn't stop her from taking it very seriously. She keeps measurements written down in her diary to compare the stats week to week as if there will be a change.

"Notice a difference?" Her eyes are full of hopeful anticipation, like a kid waiting for the ice cream man to hand over her bomb pop.

"Yes, I think you're for sure finally getting them," I say, trying not to make eye contact. "Like *totally*." I drag the last word out for emphasis.

"You're not a good liar, and I swear to God if they don't come soon, I'm going to have no choice but to buy one of those padded bras like my mom wears. I can't have Riley thinking he's dating a girl that's as flat as Kansas."

"I think that's an awful idea. Those bras are the biggest sham ever. You go out with a guy, and he thinks you have these great boobs and then when he takes your bra off, he realizes it's all a big trick. You don't want to be known as a bra stuffer," I say.

"Well, I'm screwed then. Riley's going to be excited to see under my shirt at some point, and all he's going to get is this flat nonsense." She juts out her chest toward me.

"I really think if this guy's the keeper you say he is, he'll be excited for whatever the hell you have going on under your shirt. He isn't worth a damn if the size of your chest bothers him." My smile drops, and she knows I'm not kidding. She needs to stop picking guys that only care about her looks and not everything else she has going for her.

When I was eight, I heard my dad tell a buddy that he fell for my mom because she had great knockers. Until Tessa told me what knockers were, I was confused as hell, and once I knew, it took effort to keep myself from puking. Even if my parents weren't together anymore, it's still disturbing to think of them like that.

I'm not sure why my dad's surprised that his marriage went down the toilet. You don't marry someone for her boobs and expect to find your soulmate.

After spending two hours trying on outfits and applying our make-up, we're both satisfied with how we look. I decide on a pair of bleach-splattered denim short-shorts that my dad would kill me if he knew I owned, and Tessa's gone with a short denim mini-skirt and a pink tank top with silver and black paint streaks splashed all over it.

We stand in front of Tessa's full-length mirror, double-checking our teased bangs and matching lavender eye shadow. I turn around and admire my backside and the smooth olive skin I'm naturally blessed with in the summer, and then we head downstairs to ask Tessa's mom if she can drive us to Lori's house. If my dad saw me done up like this, he would know I was doing it to attract a boy. He thinks I'm sleeping over at Tessa's and that we planned a movie marathon for the whole evening. My dad nor Tessa's mom have a clue what we're really doing tonight. Neither do I for that matter, now that I think of it.

"You girls look fabulous," Janet says, turning from a sitting position in front of the giant potted plant in her bedroom with her legs folded on top of each other. She finishes her deep breathing and stands to stretch. "Any fun plans happening tonight?" Rushing over to admire Tessa more closely, she lays a hand on her shoulder.

Tessa shrugs her off with a look on her face that implies she doesn't think Janet deserves to know our plans. "We want to go to Lori's to watch some new videos on MTV and, like, do each other's nails," she lies, barely making the effort to come up with a believable story.

Before Tessa moved, that's exactly what we'd be doing on this Saturday while sneaking some of my dad's peach schnapps. Just the two of us. Schnapps in any flavor is our favorite thing to get our hands on. My dad always has some stashed in the back of our freezer that we can sip on. It makes us feel warm and fuzzy inside—kind of like Nyquil without the medicinal effect that makes you want to sleep for a whole day. She closes her eyes in annoyance, waiting for Janet's verdict. "Well? Can you drive us to Lori's or not?"

When Tessa's rude to her mother, I want to slap her. She doesn't know how lucky she is to have a mother who cares. I'm constantly telling her I wish to hell Janet was my mom. She says I only wish for a mother like hers because my mother is on another planet and completely checked out. She tells me that if my mother was like hers, I'd be totally annoyed, too. I wish I could give it a test run to confirm this—but that's never happening.

I've lost track on how long it's been since I've even seen my mom. Not that she's keeping a record since she's gone through one boyfriend after another in the last year. My older sister Chelsea says mom wishes she was twenty-five again so she can relive the life she had before having kids. The problem is—she has kids. It's not like we're grown up and gone. I think having my brother a little over a year ago caused something to snap inside her. Her kids are no longer on her agenda.

"Of course I can," Janet says, her smile deflating from the rejection. My heart aches for her. "You girls go jump in the car, and I'll be right behind you after I let Dad know we're headed out to Lori's. Mmm-kay?"

Tessa and I start the car immediately and blast the air conditioner. We spent way too much time on our hair to have it ruined in this Missouri heat where the humidity rivals the rain forest. We're both sitting up front, sharing the seat in her mom's Honda Accord that smells like some sort of potent patchouli oil. Tessa furiously presses every button on the dash like she–knows she's missing her favorite song.

"Holy hell, it's hot." I'm angling my face in front of a vent, trying to find the perfect flow of air to save my hair from ruin. This has been the hottest summer in the history of Midwest summers that I can remember, and it's seriously cramping my style. I peek at my reflection in the passenger mirror. Yikes, my hair is already starting to get frizzy again and instead of looking like a hot Kelly LeBrock, I'm starting to feel like a poodle. I should've put it up in a side pony.

Tessa leans over to the driver's side and starts honking the horn over and over.

Janet emerges down the sidewalk, purse swinging back and forth, once again rushing to please Tessa.

"Tonight's going to be totally awesome. I can't wait to get to Lori's and lay my sweet lips on Riley's." She puckers her glossy, hot pink lips at me.

"You're completely crazy you know that?" I laugh at her, but I can feel my chest tighten at the thought of being around a bunch of guys I don't know. If my dad had even a clue that I wasn't staying at her house tonight, I'd be locked in my room until I'm eighteen.

Janet hops into the car out of breath. "What are you girls conspiring about?" She shifts from one side of her body to the other, trying to avoid having her butt cooked on the scorching hot seats.

Tessa ignores her, scanning through the radio stations until she catches the faint sound of Let's Go Crazy by Prince. She cranks the music up to the max. "Meg, it's your man." She nudges me with her body, and a smile takes over my face as the beats speak to my soul. Prince has a way of instantly switching me into party mode, and Tessa knows it. She starts shimmying her shoulders and I bop my head. "Meg, tonight's going to be so rad, just wait," she whispers in my ear. "I have a feeling everything's about to change for you."

*Oh Jesus*, I think. She's always been my saving grace when it comes to pulling me out of the slump my home life causes. Tonight, though, I think she has plans that'll do more than send me home tomorrow feeling like I can face another crappy week. If her plan for this night does change everything, I'm not sure I'm brave enough to go along with it.

She sways into me, belting out Prince while Janet concentrates on driving, her head bopping a little to the beat, too.

Tessa's changing somehow, but I can't quite put my finger on it. Now that she's going to a different school, I'm terrified of the division I feel might happen between us. I'm sick of being home every weekend watching my baby brother, knowing she's out having so much fun without me. Fear of my dad busting me has kept me prisoner at home for too long, and I'm done with it. Things have to change or I'm going to lose my mind. I must be fearless and stop always playing it so safe. It's not my plan to break all my dad's rules tonight, but that might be exactly what needs to happen.

I'm going into high school, and at what point do I get to go to parties and finally have a boyfriend like all the other girls I know? Plus, my sister thinks she's some sort of badass because she's managed to hide her boyfriend from my dad. If she can hide her social life than why can't I? Tessa keeps telling me it's time for a change, and I think I'm finally ready.

Sitting up straight, I whisper back to her, "I'm in." Whatever this surprise is, it better be pretty damn good, because if I get caught it's all over. Tessa will move onto her new life without me because my dad will make sure I'm not anywhere near anything that resembles fun or Tessa.

Tessa grabs my hand and gives it a quick squeeze. Leaning back in the seat, she closes her eyes and gets lost in the song that's still blaring at full volume. She doesn't have a worry in the world. It's like nothing can touch her, like nothing could ever bring her down.

I long for that exact feeling of freedom. I close my eyes and let the music sweep away all my anxiety. I'm ready for my life to change, too. It's about time I start living.

And I think I'm finally ready.

## Chapter Two

Letting ourselves in at Lori's, George Michael is booming from a radio in her living room. She's smoking a cigarette and sitting on the red, shagged carpeted floor, petting the belly of a wiener dog who resembles a barrel more than he does a dog. With her head titled up and her eyes closed, she's singing along with the radio—it's obvious she didn't hear us come in.

Tessa strolls over and turns the radio down.

"Hey, dudes!" Lori rocks back and forth on the floor, jumping to her feet.

I'm not sure who lives here besides Lori and her mom, but this house is bizarre with its bright tapestry covered walls and oversized furniture filling up the whole room. Lori sort of looks like E.T. with an oddly long neck and high cheek bones. She seems kind of strange, but Tessa likes her so I guess it's okay. Reminding myself I'm here to have fun, I decide to stop concentrating on Lori and the weirdness that seems to come along with her.

"Who's coming over tonight?" Tessa claps her hands together in excitement.

"Mason, Riley, Jason, and a couple of girls from Flat Burger, where Mason works."

Flat Burger is a local fast food joint in my town that's been there since my dad was a kid. They sell giant burgers that are flat and come in foil bags that you peel back as you eat your burger. And the girls who work at Flat Burger are not girls you worry about showing you up. They all look like members who belong in a fast food cult with their bleached hair, white eyeliner, and dark lipstick. To be honest, they kind of scare me. I've never understood why every single one of them does their hair and makeup the same like it's a job requirement—but they do.

"Do you guys want a beer or something?" Lori turns to us.

"Totally," Tessa and I say in unison.

Lori leads us into the kitchen and tosses us each a beer from an avocado-colored fridge that appears not to have a working light. The beer is lukewarm and tastes terrible. My dad keeps his beer super cold, and now I'm ridiculously annoyed by beer that's not up to my beer temperature standards. His motto is that you can buy cheap beer as long as you keep it ice cold. This always makes my grandma roll her eyes at him. He's right of course, even if he doesn't know that I too appreciate cold beer.

We sit outside on Lori's porch waiting for the others, sipping on our beers and sharing a cigarette. Guilt nags at me for lying to my dad about tonight. If he knew I plan to be around older boys all night, or any boys for that matter, he'd flip out. I'd be grounded for what little summer I have left. He needs to be worried about Chelsea not me—she's the one having sex these days.

By the time a couple of vehicles come pulling into the yard, I'm relaxed and ready to talk to someone else. Lori and Tessa have been blabbing about school drama that I know nothing about, which is kind of bugging me.

"You excited to meet Jason?" Lori asks, fiddling with one of the neon yellow hoop earrings dangling from her ear.

"Umm sure. Who's Jason?"

"I didn't exactly tell her," Tessa says.

"Tell me what?" I'm confused and my heart starts pounding.

"Okay, so don't freak out, but we, like, sort of told Jason that you're single and wanted to meet him."

Tessa tries to act like it's no big deal, crossing her legs and leaning back on the porch, but she knows I'm going to panic.

"You did what?" I jump up to go inside before whoever Jason is gets to the porch.

"If I told you about Jason you, like, never would have agreed to it," Tessa says, standing up beside me. "I did mention there was a boy though, remember? I just didn't tell you we already matched you up with him."

She's right, I would've backed out. I scramble inside so I don't look lame standing there like I'm dying to meet him. Who wants some guy thinking they're waiting around on some chick's porch like a puppy at the pound waiting for someone to take her home?

Heading for the bathroom to check if my hair isn't a total mess, I shut the door and lock myself inside. Adrenaline is now killing the buzz I'd been catching from the beer. My hair looks like hell, thanks to sitting on the porch. Why I agreed to sit outside is beyond me.

When I open the medicine cabinet to find some toothpaste or something to fix my breath, prescription bottles come flying out and land in the sink. I quickly stuff them all back onto the shelf, struggling to grasp them all at once. One of the items is a box of condoms. What kind of a parent keeps condoms in the hall bathroom? Actually, I bet my mother probably does, but I wouldn't know because I haven't been to her house in I don't know how long.

On the back of the toilet next to a box of tampons, which totally grosses me out, I spy some toothpaste. I don't want to be bad-beer-breath girl so I do the brush your teeth with your finger trick my grandma always has us do when we sleep over at her house. I give myself one final look in the mirror and smooth my tangle of curls down my back. The music is turned up again, and everyone is talking in the living room. I swing the door open. *Here goes nothing*, I think.

Walking out fast and with confidence holding my head high, I round the corner, slamming right into a guy, spilling his beer all over my shirt and down my legs.

"Whoa." He catches me before I fall forward onto him.

I briefly look up at him and then down at my shirt.

He smiles and says, "Well, now they don't have to introduce us." He massages the back of his neck and stares at me while I try to wipe all the beer off my arms.

"I'm Jason." He leans forward and speaks into my ear so I can hear him over the music.

"I'm drenched," I say. I start back to the bathroom to find a towel, holding my arms out in front of me like a walking zombie off *Scooby-Doo* as I drip beer all over Lori's floor.

I'm about to shut the bathroom door behind me when he dashes in and stops the door from closing with his arm.

"I saw a towel hanging in the kitchen." He glances down the hall in the direction of the kitchen. "I'll go grab it. Meet me out front?"

I nod and take a deep breath as I spin toward the living room.

I weave past Tessa and a group of girls from Flat Burger who are squatting on the floor, digging through tapes. They have them strung out all over the place while they debate on what to play next. Tessa looks up at me with a wide grin on her face. I have no clue why she's smiling so much, but I give her a quick, dismissive wave and keep walking. She turns her attention back to the tapes.

Discreetly, I go outside and sit on the tailgate of a

beat-up, old grey pick-up truck. I try to get it together before I make a complete jackass out of myself—if I haven't already. A momentary thought crosses my mind that I'm going to have to borrow something of Lori's to wear home or Janet will have a stroke when I get in her car tomorrow reeking like the local bar.

The click of the front door opening and then closing startles me. I turn and Jason is walking toward me with a bunch of napkins balled up in a fist that look like the ones you get at Flat Burger.

"Sorry. This is all I could find." He slides a hand into his front jean pocket after dumping all the napkins on the tailgate next to me.

"I thought you said you saw a towel in the kitchen?" Trying to sop up the beer as best as I can, I avoid looking at him.

"I lied because I was afraid if you went back into the bathroom again, you'd never come back out."

I stop drying off my shirt and look up at him. I'm so stunned by his eyes that I can barely think of a response. They are the color of honey. I've never seen eyes quite like them. They're light brown with gold flecks throughout, and the effect makes them sort of light up. One deep-set dimple on the right side of his face and his nose with a crooked curve to it, draw me in for a closer look at him. At first glance I think maybe his nose was broken before, but then I realize it's a perfect imperfection.

I manage to say, "Thanks."

"I also brought you a beer," he says, handing me a tepid can, grazing my fingers as he does it. My heart beats so fast, I'm afraid he can tell how nervous I am. I crack open the beer and he slides onto the tailgate next to me. I hope the beer can help calm my nerves some.

"So, Tessa tells me your last name is Shine."

"Tessa told you correct." I laugh.

"Can I call you Sunshine?" He leans one shoulder into mine.

"Not if you want me to answer," I reply.

He smiles revealing that one adorable dimple and I soften a little.

"They didn't tell you about me, did they?"

"Umm no," I say softly trying not to sound rude, like I'm not glad he's here.

"I guess I can't be a disappointment when you didn't even know you were meeting me," he says, continuing to flash an amused smile.

The sun is making its decent from the sky bringing about the time of day when you're ready for the hustle and bustle of daytime to go and the winding down that evening brings to begin. We sit there silently watching it go with nothing but the loud buzz of tree crickets in the background. It's not even awkward. It's strangely comfortable sitting beside him taking in our surroundings. Just as I'm about to ask him how he knows Lori, I hear Tessa hollering my name from the front porch in the slurring way that tells me she's had too much to drink already.

Tessa and I have a two-beer-apiece rule in a one-hour timeframe. Even though that sounds like a stupidly precise rule, it's been tested. We learned the hard way that once we hit three beers, we make complete idiots of ourselves. The only night we've ever had three beers in less than an hour was when we played Truth or Dare with one of the neighborhood boys, Brandon.

Tessa and I both ended up lifting our shirts to flash him through my bedroom screen window like the little drunks we were. He'd been supplying us beer from his dad's cooler. It was not a big deal until he blabbed about it to everyone, and my sister Chelsea said the boys in the neighborhood all knew. We vowed then and there to deny it all and never drink three beers in a one-hour timespan again. I'm now wondering if Tessa has broken that rule by the way she's trying to get my attention.

"Duty calls." I slide off the tailgate and walk to the porch to handle Tessa, conscious of the fact that he's watching me walk away. I try to walk with a cute sway, shaking my butt a little, but then I forget how I normally walk. I'm a complete spaz.

"I think we need to, like, find a ride home." She's definitely slurring, but she also has a smile on her face. "The girls in there are being totally pissy." She swings her arm, almost hitting me in the process of pointing back at Lori's house.

So that Jason can't hear the conversation, I pull her close to me and lean into her ear. "What are you talking about? Your mom thinks we're sleeping over here, and I'm not about to call her when you're drunk. How are you already this drunk, Tessa?"

She lets out a loud laugh, stumbling into me, and then sits down in the middle of the yard, while unsuccessfully trying to keep her skirt from riding up. "I made the Flat Burger chicks mad, and Lori seems to think I'm being rude. I thought I was being helpful, but I guess some people don't appreciate my advice."

The front door opens, and a boy I assume is Riley comes strolling out of it with a smirk on his face. He tells me that the Flat Burger chicks don't like to be told that they could be pretty if they basically changed everything about themselves.

Jason comes up behind me, putting his hand on my shoulder. His touch sends a current through my body that I've never known before.

"Tell me you didn't say that?" I look down at Tessa, and she shrugs her shoulders as if we're discussing someone other than her. "Well, we can't go to your house or mine," I say to Tessa, placing my hands on my hips.

"Isn't your dad like working an all-nighter?" she asks.

"Yes, but it'll take us an hour to walk there," I say.

"We can walk you," Jason offers.

"Yeah, and it will do her some good to walk off the alcohol," Riley pipes in.

"What about Lori and Mason?" I ask.

"We'll tell them we're taking a walk. Besides, I came here to see you," Jason says.

I'm thankful that it's almost dark out, because I can feel the heat rushing to my face as he says this—and I don't blush easily. Poor Tessa is so fair-skinned that she blushes from her neck all the way to her forehead.

"Yeah, they came here to see us, Meg, duh," Tessa says, and starts giggling. She topples over and we help her up.

*This is going to be a long walk*, I think.

In the back of my mind I'm terrified that my dad will catch me with guys in the house. I'm not even supposed to be home tonight. I don't want Jason thinking I'm lame, though—I hope to hell I don't get caught. Jason holds my hand for most of the walk, and soon my worries of getting in deep trouble melt away. Tessa's been jabbering on most of the way about whatever comes to her drunken mind.

When we approach my house nearly an hour later, Chelsea's boyfriend's beat up Monte Carlo sits parked up the street in a weak attempt at camouflaging that he's here. If dad comes home it won't matter who's parked where—we'll all be dead meat.

"Looks like we have Ms. Drama to deal with."

Tessa notices the car, too. Ms. Drama is what she likes to call Chelsea.

The walk has helped her a little. She's still laughing and stumbling, but at least she's making sense. We all go in the back door, and I lead us to the living room.

Chelsea comes stomping up from the basement huffing and puffing like the big bad wolf that she is. "Really Meg? Dad thinks you're at Tessa's." She narrows her eyes as she looks at all of us.

"So, where does he think you are?" I shoot back at her.

"Fine, hang up here so I can have some privacy please," she says, lowering her voice an octave into her big sister bossy tone. She looks us up and down a second time, pursing her lips—like we are the biggest losers ever.

"Don't have a cow. We didn't plan on hanging out with you anyway." Rolling my eyes, I turn away from her. Jason plops down on the puffy, brown corduroy couch that I'm used to curling up on with a book. Instead of a juicy novel, I have him to curl up with, which is a welcomed change. He pats the spot next to him for me to sit.

I go sit next to him, well aware that our legs are touching.

"Your sister's a real charmer," Jason says.

"She's not that bad as long as you do everything she says," I say.

Tessa laughs and takes Riley by the hand and leads him to our back patio.

"If you're going out there you seriously have to be quiet," I tell her. I don't want the neighbors hearing her and telling my dad we had boys over.

"Oh, we won't be doing much talking." She looks

back at Riley.

It's irritating that my best friend has become the girl who's drunk and acting like she has tons of experience with guys when she doesn't. Since she moved, Tessa has kissed a couple of guys at parties, but nothing major has happened yet. She loves to tell Chelsea all about it and get tips from her on what guys want. Also wanting the tips, I listen, but I don't want them to come from my sister. I have no other options at this point.

As I grab a deck of UNO cards off the coffee table. I hold them up to Jason. "You ready to lose to the queen of UNO?"

"Bring it on, I'm an UNO master."

"We'll see about that," I say.

I shuffle the cards like a Vegas dealer setting up a table. Grandma taught me and Chelsea to shuffle when we were little, and we're both bad ass at it.

"Geez, Sunshine, you're not messing around."

"I told you I'm the queen." I give him a playful grin.

He motions for me to deal. We sit cross-legged on the couch, facing each other with the playing cards between us. He'll be a junior this year like Chelsea, and I hope it doesn't bother him that I'm younger than he is. He isn't shocked that I live with my dad full-time either. He tells me he hasn't seen his dad since he was five. His mom works at Taco Bell and she's rarely home, so he pretty much runs his own life. Turns out I've seen her several times at Taco Bell. She seems nice enough, but a bit rugged, like she's lived a hard life.

After I obliterate him at UNO ten times, he gives up. We lounge on the couch and talk for a couple hours. At one point, he rests his hand on my leg, and my body tenses. It's like a surge of lightning moving through me.

I've got to calm down, it's his hand for God's sake. We've been talking so much that I'm surprised when Chelsea suddenly appears in the living room with her boyfriend. I forgot all about them.

"Meg, everyone needs to go. I have no clue when dad's going to show up."

She grabs her boyfriend's hand and heads to the front door as if he's a toddler being delivered to his mother.

I look at the clock in the kitchen, and I can't believe it's almost three in the morning. Standing up, I stretch my cramped legs that have been folded for way too long.

Jason reaches his arms over his head, and my stomach quivers when the small trail of hair running from the bottom of his stomach into his jeans shows like the trail of seduction it is.

He draws me into him, smoothly placing his lips on mine. His hand slides down and intertwines our fingers while he kisses me. I'm pretty sure my legs are going to give out, but I manage to keep standing. I get lost in the kiss, feeling some of the freedom I've been longing for. A little moan I didn't know I was going to let out escapes my mouth and causes him to press his whole body into mine. Kissing him for a moment longer and loving his soft lips that taste like cherry Chap Stick, I break away as the reality that my dad's coming home swims back into my mind.

"I, umm, need to go get Tessa." I look into his eyes.

"I had a great time tonight, Sunshine," he says.

"Me too," I say, totally aware that he's still holding my hand. "I better go get Tess."

She's curled up asleep with Riley in my dad's dirty, old hammock when I make my way to the patio.

"Tess, my dad could be home soon. You need to get up." I'm being stern, hoping she doesn't ignore me. I manage to shake her awake after what seems like a full minute of trying.

When she slowly opens her eyes, she has the look of a bear coming out of hibernation. Apparently, she just realized she isn't at home. She smiles and rolls out of the hammock—still in her miniskirt. Even though she's sobered up, she looks like she's been rolling around in a pen with wild animals all night. I order her to go inside while I try to figure out what to do with Riley. She pats my shoulder as if this is an average Saturday night, well Sunday morning now. I would do anything for her carefree, no worry attitude.

Jason comes outside and chuckles when he sees Riley still asleep. "I'll get him up and out of here."

Feeling the stickiness of the August air continuing its destruction on my hair, I nod and tell him thanks.

"Can I call you?" He's still staring at me with those beautiful eyes.

Turning around, I go back into the house and grab a pen off the table. Then I head back to the porch where Jason is trying to wake Riley. I take his hand and write my number on it, which is a gutsy move, and I hope I'm not making a fool of myself.

"I'll call you later," he says, and plants a soft kiss on my cheek that has an impact all the way down my body.

Jason turns to leave, and I wrap my arms around myself. I feel proud that I was bold enough to give him my number, but I wonder how I'm going to hide this from my dad.

## Chapter Three

Tessa goes into my bathroom to drown her face in my sisters Sea Breeze to get ready for bed. I need to make sure to remind her to call her mom first thing when we wake up. We don't need her mom showing up at Lori's to pick us up when we're over here. At this rate, that's going to be in like four hours. As I sit down on my bed wrestling my hair into a high pony, I replay my kiss with Jason before I'm interrupted by Tessa's big mouth.

"We, like, totally did it!" Tessa's eyes are red rimmed, but her sleepiness doesn't mask her excitement.

"We did what?" I ask.

"Not you and me we, but Riley and me we."

"What are you talking about?" I hope she doesn't mean what I think she means.

She sits down on the floor next to me. "I let him, you know, like touch me downtown if you catch my drift."

I shush her. I don't want Chelsea knowing all our business.

She looks at me for a second. "Glad you're happy for me."

"I'm not, not happy for you, I'm surprised is all."

"It kind of freaked me out at first, but then I, like, totally went with it," she says smiling from ear to ear. "Plus, my skirt kind of gave him easy access if you know what I mean." She waggles her eyebrows up and down.

"Oh my God, Tess, you're so nuts."

She stands to free her boobs from her bra, as if it's needed.

She throws on one of my t-shirts and climbs into my bed. I start to worry that Jason was bored tonight. If Tessa went that far with Riley, why didn't Jason try anything with me? Maybe I wasn't putting off the right vibe for him to pick up on. I don't even know how to put off that kind of vibe. This whole situation is going to cause me a stroke, and I'm not even an adult yet. Before my dad shows up in the morning with Zachary, I need to get some sleep. I don't know how Chelsea got out of watching my brother tonight—grandma must've volunteered to keep him. Tessa's breathing has become loud and heavy, and I realize she's already out. I climb in beside her, feeling sticky and wishing to hell we had air conditioning. In the darkness of my room, my thoughts drift back to the kiss.

****

The sound of a car door rouses me up out of a dead sleep. I jump out of bed to look out my window, wondering what time it is. I feel like I've only been asleep for an hour. My dad must've gone to the grocery store, because he's currently outside unloading bags onto the driveway and trying to calm Zachary down.

Tessa's still asleep, and I jostle her.

"What?" Her voice is muffled from under the pillow. Her head is buried under there, and she's curled in a ball.

"My dad's home. We need to go help him unload the groceries and pretend we just got here."

She lifts the pillow off her head. "Seriously?" Tessa is a complete pain in the ass to deal with when she's tired.

"Yes seriously. Now get up." I pinch my cheeks and slip on a better pair of shorts to seem more alert.

"This is like the shittiest way to wake up ever." She whines as she drags herself out of my bed.

"That's because you decided to piss Lori off and we ended up here, so move it," I say. I haul her down the hallway, hoping my dad believes Janet dropped us off here this morning. I smooth her hair down, and she slaps my hand away. Lying is a ton of work. I can't keep up with it all.

My dad is on the driveway digging through multiple grocery bags, searching for something while my brother cries at his feet.

"Gan, Gan," my brother babbles as he holds his arms up to me for a lift. His amber curls are stuck to his face with sweat. He hasn't yet been able to say Megan or he doesn't want to—so Gan it is.

Hefting him onto my hip, I kiss his wet cheeks, but this doesn't stop his wailing.

"I didn't know you girls were here." Dad whips around, raising his eyebrows suspiciously.

I want to smack Tessa for standing there rubbing her eyes and slouching over like she's still half asleep.

"Yep! Reporting for grocery duty." I lift my hand and give him a small salute, ignoring his curious sideways glance at Tessa.

He looks back at me and smirks. "I'll let you girls take over, but if you find Zach's sucker buried in there, please stick it in his mouth. He's been howling for it the whole ride home."

I put Zach down so I can start loading up grocery sacks. My dad walks off mumbling something about the idiot checker losing the sucker, and I try to balance three bags while nudging Tessa in the back with one.

She's ignores me, concentrating on plowing through the sacks of food.

I know she's looking for the cookies my dad buys. Her mom doesn't keep any sugar in their house, so she's like a crack head needing a fix at mine. My dad always says that we supply her sugar and she supplies us with an empty cookie jar. She pulls out the sucker and inspects it for a minute. Pulling a hair off the sucker, she plops it in Zach's mouth, instantly stopping his cries.

He gives her legs a hug and waddles into the house.

"Looks like this isn't payday week for your pops, because there's, like, no cookies in sight," she says.

"You'll only find the essentials this week." I'm trying not to drop all the groceries I'm balancing without her help.

My dad is currently waiting for his day in court to stop paying my mom child support. We're supposed to be at her house every other week, but she's called with an excuse when it's her turn to have us for the last year. She lives only two blocks over, but we still haven't seen her. I don't think she even calls anymore.

Dad often says, "If my damn money wasn't going to your damn mother, we could stop being so damn broke while she traipses around town spending it."

We usually get this speech when we ask for something outside of the budget, like makeup. It doesn't stop us from asking. It just sucks we have to listen to him complain about it every time.

****

Later that afternoon, once Tessa has gone home and Zachary was passed out in my dad's bed having his nap, I venture outside to my tree. With a Seventeen magazine tucked inside the waistband of my shorts, I start to climb. There's a giant oak tree with thick, sturdy branches in the backyard taller than every house on my street. I can see the roof of Tessa's old house from up here, and it's sad to look at it now knowing she isn't in there anymore.

My dad doesn't bother me when I'm up here, and Chelsea is terrified of heights. It's all mine for now, until Zach learns how to climb, but by then I'll be off to college. When my grandma is around, I try not to climb it because it sends her into a panic. She stands under it yelling, "Get down from there before you're fried to a crisp like a piece of bacon." She thinks at any moment a branch is going to touch a power line and zap me. Picturing the commercial that plays on the television, warning of just such a disaster, I keep track of the power lines when I come up here. I've climbed up here for years now. I figure I would've been zapped by now if it was going to happen.

When I look out over my neighborhood, I'm reminded of why I came up here to think. I don't want to admit to myself what I know is eating at me. It's not that I'm jealous of Tessa and Riley— it feels like it goes beyond that. Every day something changes, and I can't keep up.

One day I'm living at home with both my parents, playing outside doing hand stands on the front lawn with Tessa and Chelsea, and now we're all going in different directions. Chelsea's never home, and Tessa is leaving me behind for her new friends, and experiencing so much without me. Dad's working constantly to make ends meet, and he's exhausted most of the time.

If Jason would've actually tried to do more than kiss me, I'm not sure I would've let him. I think I need to start preparing myself for all the things Tessa's doing with Riley. I'm not opposed to it, but I'm not sure if Jason has thought about doing more—we did just meet. A sudden fluttering sensation starts in my chest as I remember that he said he'd call me later. I wish I knew when later was. With Jason going to another school and summer break being over in a week, I don't have a clue how I'll ever see him again.

I'm going to have to beg Chelsea to answer the phone every time it rings from now on so she can cover for me if Jason calls. My dad is used to her flying toward the phone like Publisher's Clearing House is calling to tell us we won a million bucks any time it rings, but if I do it he'll know something's up.

The screen door to the back porch slams, and I peep below to see my dad dragging a bag of charcoal over to the grill.

Without looking up, he says, "How about some burgers tonight, Meggie?"

"Only if you let me flip them." I make my way down the tree.

He goes back inside and comes back out carrying the Scrabble board. My dad and I have a Scrabble game going at all times. We leave the board sitting in the living room for weeks and go back to it whenever he has a free moment. He places the board on the patio table and pulls up a chair.

"Your turn," he says with a tight-lipped smile like he's got some major point heavy word brewing that I can't see.

I'm determined to nail him with a word that'll put my score over his for once. He pops his beer open and slides it to me for a sip. If I'm next to my dad when he opens a beer, he always gives me the first tiny sip and then says to me, "Now isn't that stuff awful." I always let out a giggle that makes him happy and we carry on with whatever we're doing. Little does he know that this little gesture over the years is the reason I love beer.

Seeing a slot that I can fit the word sex into, I tense up. Would he flip the board over and kill me right here on the back porch, or praise me for finding a use for the letter x? Telling my brain to knock it off, I go with the word fence, abandoning the x altogether. I would like to live another day.

We play for a while, and Zachary eventually drifts out, naked from the waist down, dragging my dad's pillow with him.

Chelsea trails right behind him holding a clean diaper. "He took his diaper off in bed again." She scoops Zachary up. "You can play as soon as you get a new diaper," she says, tucking a lock of hair behind her ear and giving him a stern look.

Zachary typically listens to Chelsea because I think he knows that she doesn't take no for an answer. Grandma and I are loosey-goosey, but Chelsea means business.

"Also, Dad, you might want to change your sheets as soon as possible. Thanks to Zach, they're now wet." She finishes taping the diaper closed.

I push the Scrabble board away. "I got this." I want to be in the house anyway so if Jason calls I can answer the phone, and this pee sheet duty gives me an excuse.

"Thanks, girls," Dad says.

He gets the grill going, and the glorious summer aroma of charcoal smokiness drifts through the house. This weekend started out depressing but has turned out to be the best weekend I've had in a long time thanks to Tessa. Friday night watching Zachary while Dad worked seemed like the start of another weekend trading off babysitting with Chelsea and being bored to tears with our routine. I owe Tessa big time for setting me up with Jason, and I'm kicking myself for not thanking her— even though she knows I'm grateful.

After eating one of my dad's yummy burgers and giving Zachary a bath, Chelsea and I decide to go to her room and paint our nails. It's easier if we paint each other's than trying to do our own.

"I think Jason is going to call anytime," I say swiping a bright turquoise color on Chelsea's thumb nail.

"Okay, geez you don't have to keep saying that. I told you if he called I'd answer. You need to stop acting like such a needy spaz about it."

*Piss off.*

"I know. Okay sorry," I say lowering my eyes back down to concentrate on her nails. I know better than to make her mad right now, and by the time we go to bed it doesn't matter. Jason never called.

## Chapter Four

The whole next week I spend with Chelsea, trying to get ready for school ... and trying to distract myself from thoughts of Jason. I didn't even see Tessa all week, which I think is a record for us.

"Seriously, Meg, get your head together. We don't have that much time, and we both need new clothes. I won't always be here to pick everything out for you," she says, and folds her arms over her chest, waiting for me to pick a store to start at.

"Do you think we have the money for me to get some purple Converse?" I don't know why I'm asking. I know we can't afford it.

"Please tell me you're kidding. No, we don't have the money for purple shoes, and your stupid infatuation with Prince is going too far if you're now wanting purple shoes," she says, rolling her eyes.

"Fine, but I don't know where to start with the little money we have. I hate the mall."

Looking around at all the shops filled with high school girls, we're trying to lay out a plan to make the money dad gave us stretch. Three hours later, after following Chelsea around trying to find every shop with a sale going on, we're finally as satisfied as we can be with our clothes. It's hard to hide the jealousy we feel at the girls trailing behind their mothers out of The Gap with arms loaded down full of sacks of new outfits.

On the walk home, I tell Chelsea about how Tessa is going further and further with guys and how Jason still hasn't called.

"If you're going to start dating you need to realize that boys play games." She's going into lecture mode.

"I don't think Jason is playing a game, and I think I might die if I don't hear from him."

She throws her arms in the air like my feelings about Jason are wearing her out. "You need to get a grip, you just met him. If you want him to call then you have to find a way to keep him interested in you. Guys have the attention span of new born babies. They can forget you in minutes."

I wonder if this means I need to do more than kiss him if I ever see him again.

\*\*\*\*

That night after eating dinner and getting Dad's approval on our clothes—which consists of him looking at every outfit and shaking his head—I finally get to talk to Tessa. She asks me to come sleep over at her house for our last weekend of freedom from homework and all of the other crap that school brings. I agree to come but warn her that I'm super bummed that I haven't heard from Jason and that I'm in a crap mood.

Tessa said that Riley told her that Jason told him that he'd been thinking of me. Why is she just now telling me this? This must have been what Chelsea was talking about with boys and their games. If Jason is thinking of me, then why wouldn't he pick up the phone and call me? Obviously, I don't understand guys.

\*\*\*\*

"I totally have a surprise for you," Tessa sings as I walk into her room the next evening. She's sitting on her bed surrounded by packages of press on nails. She draws in a sharp breath of anticipation, waiting for me to get on board with her eager mood.

"Your last surprise put me into a depression, and I hope you're not considering putting on those tacky ass press on nails. I don't care if Madonna wears them, they're tacky."

"I'm going to, like, try them out. Geez, you do need some good news," she says, and tosses the fake nails off her bed.

"Spill it then." I drop my bag of clothes on her floor.

"Jason's brother is totally picking us up tonight, and we're going to hang out over at Jason's." She jumps up and hugs me, ignoring the fact that hugs aren't my thing.

"He told Riley he wanted to see you again."

My stomach does an automatic somersault. "How do we swing this past your parents?"

"My parents are going to dinner and a movie with the neighbors. We'll, like, leave after them, and you know they'll have totally gone to bed by the time I have curfew anyways."

Thinking about this for a minute, I shriek in delight, quickly covering my mouth to conceal the noise I can't contain. "We have to get ready!" I say looking down at my ratty t-shirt and shorts.

"About time I get a smile from you," she says, retrieving the press on nails from the floor and throwing them at me.

Two hours and five outfit changes later we're finally ready. I layered my eyelashes with Tessa's new blue mascara, and I'm ready to face the night. I try telling myself to be confident and show Jason that he'll want to think twice about not calling me. I'm pushing the nerves aside and deciding to go with whatever this night might bring—or at least that's my plan.

\*\*\*\*

Jason's brother pulls up in a red, extended-cab truck that sounds like it's barely going to keep running. I catch a glimpse of Jason in the back seat as I walk to the truck, standing tall with my chest out like I'm a hot super model.

Tessa motions for me to get in the back with him

while she squeezes in the front of the truck with Riley.

"Hi," Jason says in my ear.

My entire take-charge attitude flies out the window the minute his breath tickles my neck. I can't quite manage what to say, and I'm too nervous to even look at him. Saying hi back would be the obvious choice, but I'm afraid my voice will give away my nerves. I don't want him knowing he has this effect on me.

The aroma of skunky smoke, that I know isn't from a cigarette, floats back to me. Riley lit a joint, and he's passing it to Tessa. She takes a pull from the joint, as smooth as ever twisting her glossy lips around the joint, and I can tell she's been doing this more since the last time I saw her. I get ready for my turn but make a mental note to kill her later for not telling me. Pushing aside visions of Nancy Regan's Just Say No broadcasts on television, I tell myself it's just weed.

Tessa passes the joint back to me and lifts her chin in a look that says, "Just do it and don't freak out." I put the joint to my lips and assure myself that it's like smoking a cigarette. I've been sneaking my grandma's cigarettes since seventh grade so, surely, I can handle this. Taking a couple of shorts puffs off it, like I saw Riley do, I instantly feel my throat constrict. I will myself to stay calm and not cough. Even though I try holding it in, I still end up coughing a little. To my surprise, Jason's brother Kenny cheers me on.

"Yeah, smoke up!" He bangs his fist on the steering wheel with enthusiasm.

"I'm trying." I say, laughing and coughing at the same time.

We each take another couple of puffs off the joint before getting to Jason's house. When we pull up, I'm surprised to see his mom sitting on the front stoop outside the tiny brick home. She's drinking a beer and reading a book. It appears to be one of those cheesy romance novels you see for twenty-five cents at the thrift store around the corner.

Browsing in that thrift store is one of my favorite things to do. My grandma and I have wasted whole Saturday afternoons digging through old treasures in there. Thrift stores are a glimpse into the lives of strangers you'll never meet. All the old dishes with crazy patterns are rad. You can find silverware that nobody makes anymore, and I sometimes think about buying some. But my dad would view it as me bringing someone else's junk into the house, and we already have plenty of our own junk.

"Oh, your mom's home." Somehow the words are coming out of my mouth in slow motion.

Even though I know I should feel panicky about meeting his mom completely high like this, I'm pleasantly at ease. My feet feel farther away from my body than they normally do when climbing out of the truck.

"My mom's cool," Kenny says, turning to look back at me.

Jason grabs my hand and shuts the truck door behind me. His soft but firm hand sends a thrill through me as we walk to the porch.

"You guys must've been smoking something, Jase," Jason's mom says as she sweeps a strand of her long, straggly blonde bangs out of her eyes.

Her voice is raspy or maybe it's not and I'm just high. I wait for her to say something else so I can confirm if her voice does sound weird. For a moment, I also wonder who Jase is, and then I understand she's talking to Jason. This makes me laugh, and they all turn to look at me.

"What makes you think we've been smoking

something?" Kenny says back to her while cracking up at me.

"Hi," I finally say to his mom.

"You look like you could use a cigarette." She hands me one from the pack sitting next to her on the porch and looks down at her book. Yep, there it is. Her voice is weird and raspy.

I put the cigarette she just gave me in my mouth. Whose mom offers you a smoke? It's the best cigarette I've ever had. The smoke feels like silk floating in and out of my lungs.

"Smoking menthol cigarettes is bitchin when you're high," Kenny says to me as Jason leads me into the house. Kenny is strangely intense about things, and I'm not sure why.

It's dark inside the house, and I can't see anything like I'm walking into a movie theater with dim lighting that your eyes haven't adjusted to yet. Guided only by a light at the end of the hall, we shuffle into Jason's room. It smells like vanilla and something slightly stale at the same time. Instead of a bed, he has an old, dark green couch pushed against one wall and a mattress on the floor on the other side of the room.

The mattress is not the kind you put on a bedframe. It's more like the camping mattresses we used when my dad tried to send Chelsea and me to Girl Scout camp. We were only at the camp one night when Chelsea threw the biggest fit about having to use the outside bathrooms, and my dad was called to come get us both. My dad gave up on us being Girl Scouts once he realized that we had to sell those cookies, and it's mostly the parent's job. I'm a little confused as to why Jason doesn't have a real bed and then it dawns on me that maybe they can't afford one—and I thought I was poor.

The off-white walls in Jason's room are covered

with The Cure and Ozzy Osbourne posters, which is a strange mix, but I like that.

"Hey, isn't that the guy that bites the heads off bats at his concerts?" I say, pointing at the Ozzy poster.

"You bet your ass it is!" Riley pumps his fist in the air.

Did he say I bet my ass? What the hell does that mean? I look over at Tessa, and she erupts with laughter. I'm now dying of laughter too.

Jason tugs me down onto the couch, and I land right in his lap.

"These girls have had enough weed for one night," Jason says, pulling me back into a hug.

In the ashtray that's sitting on a little metal table by his couch, I put my cigarette out. I calm down a little, but I still have a giggle going. "Your mom is very chill. My dad would've picked me up by my neck and killed me if I came home high."

"Yeah. She's the go-with-the-flow type."

I notice that Tessa is lying on the mattress with Riley and they're making out.

Jason reaches over, turns his lamp out, and flips his clock radio on. "That's better," he says, turning me to face him.

Feeling his mouth on mine I try to concentrate on kissing him, but it's like I'm watching us kiss frame-by-frame instead of being the one doing the actual kissing.

Tessa lets out a little snicker and then a playful slap comes from the floor.

I feel like I'm floating above the room, watching us all like we're acting out a scene in a movie. Pot really does alter your mind, I think—and then I think it funny that I even thought that. There's a glow coming into the room from the window, and I see that Jason's eyes are open.

He stops kissing me and says, "Do you want to lay down and get comfy?"

"Okay," I whisper.

We get up, and he lays down on the couch, leaving me space to lie down next to him so that I'm facing him. As I lay down, Riley leads Tessa out of the room. I briefly wonder where they're going and then my brain freaks out, and for a split second I picture my dad barging in the room. I tell myself he has no clue where I am and to get it together.

"I'm glad you wanted to come over tonight." Jason pulls me out of my thoughts.

Suddenly feeling gutsy, I start kissing him first this time. After a second or two, he moves his hand over my chest, and I'm melting into his body. He moves his hand inside my shirt, undoing my bra. Pushing my body against him, I can feel his hardness through his jeans at my bellybutton. Moving my hand slowly down I begin to go for the button on his jeans.

"I wouldn't do that if I was you," he whispers against my lips.

I'm clearly tormenting him, but also unsure in the back of my mind. Kissing him is like the most addictive thing I've ever experienced. The more he kisses me, the more I begin to wrap my body around his.

The next thing I know, he has my skirt pulled up and my underwear pushed to the side. He slowly gets up and undoes his jeans. Then he lays back down next to me. I'm aware that things are now going further then I'm ready for. He pushes his underwear down, and rolls on top of me.

"I have to have you right now."

He positions himself between my legs, my underwear still pushed aside, and reality comes to me.

"I've never done this before," I say.

"I'll be gentle. I promise."

"We don't have a condom, and I don't think I'm ready for this," I say, trying to convince him we shouldn't, but praying he doesn't hate me for it.

"I'm guessing you're not on the pill?"

Unable to speak, I shake my head no.

"I can get a condom, and I'll only go in a little," he begs against my ear.

At that moment, there's a knock at the door. I freeze, and my earlier thought of my dad comes back to me.

"Jase, I'm hitting the hay. You need to turn down that radio," his mom says through the door.

I'm trembling for fear she'll open the door and find us mostly naked. This is nuts. I wiggle my way into a sitting position. My skirt is currently up around my waist, and I pull it down and snap my bra back together.

Getting the hint, Jason pulls on his pants and turns the radio down.

"Mood killer," Riley say from another room down the hall.

"I heard that," his mom says as she walks away.

I stand up and teeter. I'm dizzy from the pot we smoked. "I'm going to go to the bathroom really quick." I'm also wondering where the hell Jason's mom went. I don't want to run into her.

He stands up with his pants still undone and kisses me.

The kiss almost sends me right back down onto his couch. I know I need to go find Tessa before I go too far. I break away from him, but he grabs my wrist before I go.

"Hey, I'm sorry if that was too much for you. I shouldn't have pressured you like that. Forgive me?"

"Of course," I say. It's sweet of him to recognize

how I might be feeling right now even if I don't know how I'm feeling right now.

Tessa is coming out of the bathroom as I race down the hall like a crazy person trying to avoid his mom. I shove her back in the bathroom, shutting the door behind us before she even sees me coming. The bathroom catches me off guard. The room is completely and totally orange. There's an orange rug on the floor with an orange shower curtain. There's even an orange, fluffy carpet thing draped over the top of the toilet lid. A picture on the wall is a huge orange flower, and the paint on the walls is even a shade of orange.

"Tess, am I so high that everything I'm seeing is orange?"

"It's awful, isn't it?" she says, looking from one wall to the other.

Snapping out of it, I sit down on the toilet lid. "I almost did it—like all the way did it!"

"I know! Me too! And if his mom wouldn't have knocked on Jason's door, I like totally would have." She stands in front of the bathroom mirror and fluffs her hair back into its normal state.

"Wait, what? Where were you?"

"In here, in this orange creamsicle wonderland," she says, gesturing around the bathroom.

I look at her in disbelief. Why the hell were they almost going to do it in a bathroom?

"We need to sober up and keep it together until we can get home and talk to Chelsea about all this."

"Okay, okay. You're right." She nods.

We walk out of the bathroom to find Jason and Riley in the kitchen eating what looks like fish sticks, and it almost makes me gag.

"You hungry, Sunshine?" Jason is holding up a limp fish stick while Riley is gobbling a plateful.

I shake my head no, because all I can think about is the fact that we almost had sex five minutes ago.

"We need to get home." Tessa snuggles up to Riley and kisses his cheek.

Jason comes over, wraps his arms around me from behind, and whispers in my ear, "When do I get to see you again?"

I don't answer him. I lean my head back into his chest and he kisses my head. It's hard to engage in any type of conversation with him when my emotions are all over the place.

He lets go of me, eyeing me while he walks out of the room. We all follow him out to the front porch where his brother is sitting with a girl I didn't see earlier. She has beautiful black hair that's pulled into a French braid trailing down her back. She's digging through her purse and looks up when we all pile out onto the porch. She's that girl who doesn't need makeup or hairspray, but still looks absolutely gorgeous.

"Can you take us to run the girls home?" Jason is looking at Kenny, but Kenny looks blitzed out of his mind.

Jason looks down at the girl sitting on the porch. "Hey, Sanchez, want to do me a favor?"

She looks up at me and Tessa with her face set in a neutral non-judgmental expression.

"Yeah, I can take them because evidently someone smoked all my cigarettes and clearly your brother is out of it right now." She gestures to Kenny.

I look over at Jason's brother, and he looks drunk or high or something.

"I would drive Kenny's truck, but it breaks down half the time. I owe you one," Jason says to her.

"You actually owe me more than one, but okay sure we'll go with that." She folds her arms and smiles.

I walk over and stand beside him.

"Are you not going with us?"

He kisses me and tells me he's going to stay here and get his brother settled into the house. Not quite understanding why he has do this for his eighteen-year-old brother, I nod my head.

The girl whose first name I don't even know signals us toward her small white car. Tessa hops into the back, and I sit up front. We pull out of the driveway, and I notice that Jason and Riley are both trying to talk to Kenny, but he seems to be ignoring them.

"Is he going to be okay?" I'm still looking back at the porch as we pull away.

She looks at me and then back to the road. I can tell she's deciding how to respond. "Yeah, he's had too much."

I don't ask her what he's had too much of.

"I'm Lindsey, by the way."

"I'm Megan."

"Oh, I thought your name was Sunshine," she says with a smirk, and I immediately relax.

She asks me where she's taking us. Once I tell her, she starts explaining that she used to date Kenny, but they're only friends now. She must've known that I was going to ask why they broke up, because she tells me that she could no longer deal with his drama on a daily basis.

"Is he the jealous type?" I ask.

"It isn't that. He can't seem to get out from under his dope problem long enough to do something with his life. I love him, but I don't want to date someone who has zero plans for the future and is content with doing drugs with his mom all night, every night."

"Is he going to college this year?"

"He barely graduated high school with me doing all his homework, so that would be a no. Look, I know

Jason likes you, but you seem like a girl with a good head on her shoulders. I don't think you want to get mixed in with this family." She glances at me sideways, wondering how I'll react to what she just said.

"I think his mom's cool." I look out the window away from her, trying not act overly sensitive.

"Yeah, it's real cool to have a mom that sends you out to get drugs and then shares them with you like its normal to get messed up with your kid."

"Jason isn't like that though?" I say in a sort of question, turning to face her.

"He's headed in the same direction Kenny went in, and that isn't some girl's dream guy, let me tell you."

"Well, I don't want to give up on Jason because his mom and brother are potheads."

"It's much deeper than weed. I'm only warning you. You can do what you want," she says, shrugging it off.

I look back, wondering why Tessa isn't adding her two cents. She's passed out with her mouth open. We drive a little longer in silence until we reach Tessa's house. Leaning back, I give her leg a shake. She mumbles something as we get out of the car and starts walking slowly up her driveway.

"Thanks for the ride." I say, leaning in the passenger side window.

"Think about what I said okay? I can tell you're not one of them." I step away and she quickly puts the car in reverse. Waving goodbye, I wonder what in the hell I've gotten myself into.

## Chapter Five

School started Monday, and even though I dread being in school for another year without Tessa, it turns out to be a good week. My classes line up nicely unlike last year's nightmare. I had gym fourth hour, right before lunch. Every day I went to lunch looking like a total greaser. Might as well have called me Ponyboy Curtis with the way my hair was slicked down.

The whole idea of gym is stupid and quite honestly reckless on the part of the school. What the heck are they thinking? Having us climb a rope to the top of the gym ceiling with only a thin, blue gym mat to catch us if we fall? Also, I don't see the point of swinging your body through uneven bars. Is that skill going to come in handy in my future, because I'm thinking all that it's good for is a dislocated shoulder. I don't get it. This year, though, I have gym the last hour of the day, and I'm beside myself with happiness. I can go home after almost breaking a limb in gym and take my shower. I'm determined to keep my perfect GPA now that I'm in high school, and this is going to make it so much easier.

Chelsea freaked out when I told her about my night at Jason's house and said she's going to tell Dad if I don't stay away from him. I know she won't tell because I have way too much dirt on her. She's just worried I'm in over my head—she's right and it feels glorious.

I desperately miss Tessa. Chelsea's been hogging the phone, so I've barely talked to her. Even my dad's been yelling about the phone being tied up. With my grandma's urging, he decided to pay for call waiting, which is a freaking miracle. However, just because we have call waiting doesn't mean Chelsea will click over and answer the incoming call. If she's talking to her boyfriend, she could care less who's calling in. President Reagan himself could call, and she'd ignore it.

****

"I totally hate school, like hate it," Tessa says, picking at her nails as she sits on my bed Friday night. "Every teacher is out to get me this year. Why the hell do I need to learn algebra? Like really, someone needs to tell me why that shit matters."

"It makes you well rounded. You learn things about every subject so you can solve problems in multiple areas of life, not just one."

She looks at me and laughs. "This is why I love you. You come up with answers to my gripes that sound like they make total sense, even if they don't."

"Hey, my answers are legit."

"If you say so. Also, Jason told Riley you're like blowing him off, which I wanted to ask you about, but you haven't called me back all week."

Looking around the corner to make sure my dad can't hear, I say, "Wait, what are you talking about?"

"He told Riley that he's called several times, and Chelsea tells him that you're, like, busy and to stop calling. She also told me she'd have you call me when she got off the phone every night I've called. I knew it was bullshit."

"It is bullshit because I never knew either of you called."

"Call waiting," we say at the same time.

I'm going to kill Chelsea when I see her.

"Do you have his phone number?" I ask her. "I never asked him for his number because I was trying to play hard to get, but now I'm freaking out, and I want it."

"No, but I can totally get it," she says.

"Okay, when my dad goes to bed, I have to call him." I blow out my cheeks and let out a long sigh. I have hours until I can call him.

I'm happy he called but totally pissed I didn't get to talk to him. I feel panicky that he might give up on dating me and find a girl he doesn't have to work so hard to see or even talk to for God sakes. I rub my temples, feeling the beginning of a headache coming on, and Tessa can tell I'm thinking too much.

"Hey, let's take a walk down by the creek. I'm totally dying for a cigarette, and I brought us a treat." She curls her lip into a sneaky sneer.

We go out to the back patio where my dad's busy using a large, yellow shovel to place the sand that is thrown out of Zachary's sandbox back in it. My brother likes to fill up his shovel with sand and then dump it out of his sandbox until the box is completely empty. My dad lets him because it keeps him occupied for a good hour at least.

By the time my brother turned one, I was sure about three things: he is a huge pain in the ass, we all love him with every ounce of our being, and my dad is totally clueless about toddler boys.

Zachary is happily slurping on a sucker, squatted down, lining up his cars on the patio. I swear the kid has a sucker in his mouth during every waking hour. If I don't start insisting on sugar-free suckers his teeth will rot out before he even gets them all.

He looks up and reaches his arms out to Tessa. He loves Tessa, and she thinks of him as a little brother because she doesn't like kids all that much. She lifts him up, plants a kiss on his head, and turns around frowning. "He's totally stinky."

"Ugh. Okay, let me change him before we go." Taking him from her, I go in to get a clean diaper.

His bangs are hanging down in his face and I brush them out of his eyes as I lay him down on the couch to change him.

"You need a haircut buddy," I say, wiping his bottom.

"Ucky," he says around his sucker.

"You're a stinky boy." I grab his foot and nibble on it playfully.

When he squeals with delight, I can see my mom in his smile. He's the only one of us who looks like her, and I sometimes catch a glimpse of her high, cheeky grin spread over his baby face. It makes me sad, and I wonder how a smile from a toddler can make me feel so damn empty.

I sling him onto my hip after stuffing him back into his shorts. Tessa and dad are still out back, and I can see that Tessa is rambling on while he cleans up the sand. She has no clue how much he doesn't care for her anymore because she loves my dad. Ever since my dad taught her to ride a bike when we were little, she's adored him. Tessa's dad isn't a dad who goes outside with his kids to do these things. Tessa knows how to throw a Frisbee, dribble a basketball, and catch softballs, all thanks to my dad. I'm fairly certain she sort of idolizes him.

I put Zachary down on the patio in front of his cars, and he busily resumes playing.

"Dad, Tess and I are going to take a walk around the neighborhood."

His shoulders are tense and he's dumping the last of the sand into the box. He looks me up and down for clues that I'm up to something more than just taking a walk. He knows we're up to something, but what can he do? After a long week at the electric company, he's worn out. He's been overseeing a new crew and working around the clock. I know that by Friday nights, he has zero energy and wants to put Zachary to bed, enjoy some beers, and listen to his albums, hoping to hell he doesn't get called in.

"Be back by dark, and stay away from your mother's house." He rubs his forehead with the back of his hand and tosses the shovel into the sandbox.

Last week, I overheard him telling my grandma that he and Zachary were at the grocery store when he saw my mom. He was in the parking lot trying to coax Zachary out of the cart when he heard her laugh. She was walking into the Chinese restaurant next door—holding the hand of a guy who looked like he was twenty. He told my grandma that here he was, trying to juggle Zachary and groceries to feed her kids, and she's flitting about with some young punk. It worries me because I heard anger in his voice and what sounded like hurt on top of it.

My grandma's usual response to all things that involved complaining was, "The good news is that someday this will all be over … and the bad news is that someday this will all be over." My dad always walks away shaking his head in response. I mean what kind of comeback can you come up with to a truth like that?

I nod to my dad, striding out of the backyard with Tessa following. Discussing my mom is not something I want to deal with.

"Man, he seems totally pissed," Tessa says, once we get onto the street and away from the house.

"Yeah, apparently my mom is still dating that prick, and I think my dad might kill him."

"He should kill her instead. That'll totally solve the problem from happening again."

I shoot her a look, clenching my jaw.

She cringes inwardly. "Sorry, I know she's your mom, I just, like, hate what she's doing to you guys."

"I know, but she's been this way for a while now. There's no point in giving a crap." I wave my hand in the air, dismissing the whole idea of her being a mother.

"Well, I have something to cheer you up." She pulls a joint out of her pocket like it's no big deal and holds it out to me as if it's a stick of gum and not illegal drugs.

"Tess! Good grief, we're going to get caught!" I take the joint and shove it in my pocket, looking around for anyone who might see us.

"Oh, calm down. It's just weed."

"It's just going to get us busted with the cops, or worse, someone will tell my dad."

A mischievous giggle escapes her, and we head toward the creek. I swear, she has no fear and it's because she's never had a real punishment in her life.

We get to the spot by the creek that's covered with trees and overgrown rose bushes. Tessa lets out a long exhale slouching her shoulders in relaxation as we slip our shoes off and sit down on the creek bank. Dangling our feet in the ice-cold, crisp water sends a jolt of happiness through me as I think back to all the years we've been doing this. My grandma has always warned us not to put any part of our body in the creek because of leeches, but we've never seen one. I'm sure we would've had one stuck on us by now.

"Where'd you get this anyway?" I hand her the joint while she digs in her pocket for a lighter.

She takes a puff and passes it to me. "I got it from Lori. She brings them to school and, like, sells them in the bathroom."

"That's sort of messed up," I say.

"What's messed up is she totally gets the weed from her mom."

"No shit?" I look at her in shock.

"No shit." She nods and smoothly blows smoke from her mouth.

We sit there taking turns smoking and watching a large turtle dodge rocks as it floats down the creek.

"I'm going to have sex with Riley," she blurts out of nowhere.

"Are you being serious, or is this the weed talking?"

"Both." She leans toward me smiling.

We immediately lose it. I press a hand to my throat trying to stop laughing long enough to say something about her making such a big decision. Tessa is on the ground, rolling around, holding her stomach, and cracking up. We keep looking at each other, which only causes more laughter.

Finally, she sits up, wipes away tears, and pulls a stray leaf from her hair. "No, but seriously, I think I'm ready." She's hunched over, holding her stomach, trying to recover from the fit of hilarity that took hold.

"I don't know, Tess, there's a lot to think about."

"Riley and I have discussed it, and he'll use a condom, so don't, like, freak out."

I think about this for a minute. "Then I say go for it. Sex that boy up!" I hold my hand up in a high five, and she looks at me, and then up at my hand, and we lose it all over again.

We stay at the creek until we can see the streetlights creating a glow behind us.

"Hey, we need to go before my dad wonders what the hell we're doing. Let's take the long way so we can pass by my mom's. I want to see if that prick she's dating is over there."

"What would be the point of that?" Tessa furrows her brow in concern.

"There's no point, I just want to see." I look at her, and I think she gets it.

"If you're sure that it's not going to bother you."

She stands and puts her hand out to pull me up.

Sharing a cigarette on the way over, I still can't get past how good it feels to smoke a cigarette after a joint. I tell Tessa how great it is, and she gives me a look and says, "You're a total weirdo."

We approach my mom's house, and a black, shiny convertible is parked in her driveway.

"Okay, well he's obviously here and now you know. Let's head to your dad's before he wonders where we are," Tessa says.

I think she's afraid of my reaction since I'm sure the anger I'm experiencing right now is written all over my face. I'm so pissed I feel like I have actual steam shooting off my body. This guy is the reason I don't have a mother anymore. Just then, a guy comes out with spiked, black hair, a tank top, and shorts on. He looks like he just finished lifting weights or something. He's young and fit. He roots around in his car for something and goes back in the house.

The anger inside me rages, and I run toward her neighbor's yard with such purpose that Tessa chases after me.

"Meg, what are you doing? Megan? Meg?" She slows her pace, leaving me to go alone.

The last thing on my mind is consequences. My mom's neighbor has a Great Dane that shits bricks. Taking my shirt off, leaving only my tank top layered under it, I use it to pick up a huge piece of dog shit.

I stroll right over to the prick's car and wipe the shit all over his seats using the wax on wax off motion that Daniel-san learned in *The Karate Kid*. I'm getting it in there good. Mr. Miyagi would be proud as hell.

"*Run!*" Tessa yells from the street.

Looking back at my mom's door, I see the prick charging for me.

"Hey, what are you doing? Stop right now! Get over here!" he shouts.

Tessa cuts through the neighbor's backyard, and I run like hell trying to lose him.

Tessa and I know this neighborhood like the back of our hands and the darkness is working in our favor. Running like I've never run before, I charge through the brush of Mr. Banks' overgrown backyard and hop his fence. I don't stop until I'm three streets over. Glancing back, I realize he's gone.

Bent over with her hands on her knees in the middle of the street, Tessa is gasping for air. "I don't know when he gave up, but damn, I've never moved that fast."

"You know what sucks?" I say, huffing and puffing to catch my breath.

"What?"

"I loved that shirt, and I might've peed my pants a little."

She comes over to me and pulls me into a side hug as we start the walk back to my dad's.

"The look on your face when you saw him coming was classic. It's like you had a bull coming for you down the streets of Spain."

"He might have scared me, but he couldn't catch me. What a loser," I say.

"Total loser," Tessa agrees.

****

Chelsea got home from her friend Erica's and we told her all about it. After she gave it some thought, she agreed that the guy deserved it. She isn't always on board with our pranks, but she must've heard Dad complaining about this boyfriend recently, too.

Tessa called and got Jason's phone number for me once dad and Zachary went to bed. Sneaking down to the basement to call Jason, I leave Chelsea and Tessa to watch David Letterman without me. Even though we've been practically naked together, I'm nervous to actually call his house. Here goes nothing.

"Hello?"

*Oh, hell it's his mom.*

"Hi … is Jason home?"

In her strange, gruff voice, she says, "He's never home on a Friday night."

*I guess I'm a loser because I am.*

"Okay, can you tell him Megan called?"

"He told me to tell you if you called that he'll be home at eleven thirty. He went to help Riley fix somebody's tire."

"Okay, thanks."

"Bye now." She coughs into the phone like she's had bronchitis for fifty years.

"Bye."

I'm filled with happiness that he cared enough to leave a message with his mom for me. Guessing I can't sit by the phone for an hour and a half, I go back upstairs. Tessa is French braiding my sister's hair, gabbing away. Sometimes they seem more like sisters than her and I do, and I'm honestly okay with that—Tessa needs it.

We finish Letterman and share some schnapps. By the time eleven thirty rolls around I'm dying to talk to Jason, but I don't want to seem lame and call right at eleven thirty. I wait out the longest fifteen minutes of my life before I drag the living room phone to my room. Tessa climbs in my bed with a magazine, and I go into my closet and plop down on the floor, leaning against my hanging clothes. I don't want my dad hearing me on the phone. I dial his number again.

It rings only once.

"Sunshine?"

"Jason? How'd you know it was me?"

"I didn't, but I was hoping by acting like it was you, it'd be you. Look at me, I'm a badass magician."

"Haha, well hi," I say.

We talk until three in the morning. I think Tessa passed out around one, because that's when the snoring started. My legs are cramped from sitting in my closet all night, and it feels good to climb in bed. Trying to drown out Tessa's snores, my mind wanders to my conversations with Jason. I think I know what falling in love feels like now. It's like how Samantha felt about Jake Ryan in *Sixteen Candles*. She's falling for him but doesn't think she can have him. Love is terrifying.

## Chapter Six

"Eat! Eat!"

Tessa and I unsuccessfully try to sleep through Zachary yelling and jumping on my bed.

In the hopes that he'll move on to Chelsea or go back to my dad, we try to ignore him but have no such luck. He's not going away until I get up.

"All right, all right. I'm up!" I throw back my blanket and drag myself to a sitting position while Tessa remains sprawled out on the bed.

I mosey into the kitchen with Zachary trailing behind me. He's recently learned to gallop, and he's breathing heavy, bumping into my legs all the way down the hall. He only has a diaper and a t-shirt on, which he's already managed to get wet all down the front.

I see why Zachary woke me up. My dad's rocking out on the living room floor. His headphones are attached to his stereo, and he's oblivious to the fact that we're standing right behind him. I'm happy that he's having a moment of pure rock-and-roll bliss—air guitar and all—but I'd rather be in bed.

In the kitchen, I look for some cereal or something that will pacify my brother so I can return to my room and go back to sleep. We have some Cheerios, but of course, in true Shine family fashion, we don't have milk. I decide to pour some water on the Cheerios and top them with some sugar instead of dragging out the toaster.

Zachary's in his highchair, which he has totally outgrown, slamming his fists down and waiting for me to bring his cereal over.

I set the bowl of cereal down in front of him.

He looks at it for a minute—you can tell he knows something isn't quite right with it—but he decides to dig in. He takes his first bite, looks up, and smiles.

I'm relieved, because I'm not in the mood for a fit.

I tap my dad on the shoulder as I head back to my room, pointing back to the kitchen.

He pauses and then keeps on jamming to a beat I can't hear.

There's whispering coming from under the blankets, and I'm starting to realize getting more sleep isn't in the cards for me today. Tessa's on the phone, but I can't make out what she's saying. Lifting the blankets to crawl in, I'm momentarily stopped by a wall of her morning breath, and I want to gag.

She puts her hand over the receiver and tells me it's Riley. She tells Riley she's gotta go, but that she will totally make it happen. She hangs up the phone and leans into me. "You, like, better find a way to sleep over at my house tonight, because we're going to meet the guys. Jason is dying to see you. What did you guys talk about all night?" She raises one eye brow at me.

"Everything!"

"Oh man, you like got it bad for Jason." She's teasing me and pokes me in the chest.

"I know, and I'm totally freaking out." I rub my fingers into my temples to calm myself.

"Well, don't freak out because from the sound of it he totally has it bad for you, too. Geez, don't you two know how to play hard to get?"

"Oh yeah, you really look like you play hard to get with Riley." I laugh.

Under all the excitement I'm having right now, I'm scared, too. I know what we almost did last time, and I wasn't ready. I need to prepare myself for how I want things to proceed with Jason. Tessa has made up her mind to have sex, and maybe I need to do the same.

Jason and I haven't made our relationship official though, and I need to wait for that before I decide. I'm not some easy girl who will have sex with him just because he wants me to.

"Hmm…. Okay, I'll tell my dad that your parents are having family over for dinner, and they asked me to join. Can your mom come get us soon so we can get ready over there? I don't want my dad wondering why I'm doing my hair and makeup for a family dinner at your house." I lift the blankets off our heads. I can't take anymore of her breath.

"Let's stick around here for a while and, like, help with your brother. Helping out will butter him up when you ask him to stay over."

"Good thinking."

She knows how my dad operates. I also think that as much as I love to be at Tessa's for some parental normalcy, she gets some sort of family life from my house. My house gives her a brother she can play with and a sister who, while bitchy, is still sisterly and protective of her. I think Tessa feels alone at her house. My house doesn't give much opportunity to be alone—I have to climb a damn tree to get my privacy.

\*\*\*\*

We spend the next couple hours at the park with Zachary. There's a tiny playground at the baseball fields around the corner from my house. He loves the toddler swings there, and it's a good way to keep him busy without having to run around trying to contain him. The delight on my dad's face, as he watched us push the stroller down the driveway, is worth the pain in the ass it is to take my brother to the park.

\*\*\*\*

"Where are we going tonight and how?" I give Zachary another push on the swing.

"Riley said he'd meet us at the pool by my house at, like, seven. I can tell my mom we're going to meet some neighborhood girls and hang out."

It's getting easier and easier to do whatever we want at Tessa's house.

By the way Zachary is chewing on the swing's chain, I'm guessing he wants his lunch. Lifting him out of the swing to put him back in his stroller is not easy when he's kicking his legs in protest.

Tessa's ready for him though, and she plops torn up pieces of a cheese sandwich and his chewed-up, yellow sippy cup in his lap.

He calms down when he sees it's time to eat. I'm hoping when we get home, he'll take a long nap, and I can pack my stuff to go to Tessa's without bothering my dad. Every time Zachary takes a bite, he holds his food up to Tessa to give her a taste. She bends down and pretends to take a bite and chew it up sending him into cackles of happiness.

"Okay, buddy, it's time for a walk," I tell him after he finishes eating.

"No, no, no. Play Gan." He tries to get out of the stroller.

"We can come back and play tomorrow. Be a good boy, okay?"

He's still struggling to get out of the stroller when I start pushing it forward. He sits back sucking on his sippy cup when he realizes that I'm not going to stop pushing it.

We stop at 7-Eleven so Tessa can get some smokes. Her parents give her a huge allowance, and I have no clue what she does to earn it. They'd be shocked to know that it's always spent on cigarettes and junk food—or maybe they wouldn't be.

Zachary falls asleep on the way there, and I'm

hoping this doesn't derail his future nap.

Tessa goes into the gas station while I wait outside with my brother.

I see the giant Slurpee come out of the store before I even see her. She can barely carry the drink that's the size of a bucket with the paper sack she's holding. As she extends her arm out for me to grab the Slurpee, I eye the sack.

"Is Greasy Greg gift wrapping your smokes these days?" I take a big suck off of the Slurpee straw and laugh.

She walks ahead of me, out of the parking lot, grinning. Starting back toward home, she opens the sack and pulls out a box of condoms.

I stop pushing the stroller and stand there in disbelief.

"What the hell are you doing buying condoms?"

"You should've seen the look on Greasy Greg's face when I put them on the counter. His face kind of looked like yours does now." She hands me the box.

It's like she's handed me a bomb or something— like my hand is going to explode holding this box. I'd get locked in my room forever if I got caught holding a box of condoms. Throwing them at her like we're playing a round of hot potato, I'm still stunned.

She catches them and tucks the box into her waistband, pulling her shirt down.

I swear, she's the most daring person I know.

"Seriously, why would you buy those?" I tug my shirt down like I'm concealing condoms too.

"I told you, I'm going to have sex with Riley, and I, like, want to be ready."

"Well, won't he have the condoms?"

"I don't know, but remember Chelsea told us that we should totally be prepared."

Oh, great. She's quoting my sister now.

"I don't think she meant you should go buy condoms."

"Well you never know, and I don't want one of those to take care of." She points down at a sleeping Zachary who has drool dripping from his mouth.

****

Once we got home, Zachary was in full-on nap mode. I manage to carry him up the stairs and lay him onto my dad's unmade bed that's piled high with a dozen blankets. I'm satisfied that we achieved our mission to wear the kid out. I back out of the room slowly and silently shut the door.

As my dad comes down the hall, he gives me a thumbs up. I whisper to him that Tessa's mom has invited me over for dinner and ask if I can stay over there tonight. He nods, and I tell him we'll ride our bikes over there since Zachary's in a playground coma on his bed. A look of gratitude washes over his face as the tense lines across his forehead disappear. As usual, Tessa's plan has worked like a charm.

Tessa's in my room already busying herself with packing my bag. It's nice to have a friend that knows exactly what you'd pack to get ready at their house. She stuffs the condoms into her backpack, and I shudder at the thought of my dad seeing them. I haven't seen Jason for a couple of weeks and just seeing those condoms makes me feel all dizzy with longing.

We decide to abandon riding bikes and just as I'm about to have Tessa call Janet to give us a ride, Erica pulls into the driveway to pick up Chelsea. We scurry outside to beg her for a ride to Tessa's. Even though Erica's car looks like it came straight from a demolition derby, it will still get us where we need to go.

I'm relieved that the mugginess of August is

gone, and we are moving into late September weather, but I'm over riding my bike to Tessa's. My hair couldn't take another minute of humidity. I don't want Jason to think I normally resemble a chia pet.

"No way are we taking you all the way to Tessa's house. Its way out of our way," Chelsea says.

I flinch at how she can be so cold to me sometimes when I'm not even trying to upset her.

Ignoring Chelsea, Tessa looks at Erica. "I think this will totally change your mind." She holds up five one-dollar bills, fanning herself with them and batting her eyelashes.

Chelsea turns to look at Erica, expecting her to turn us down despite Tessa's attempts to make her and Erica laugh.

"Get in," Erica says.

Chelsea rolls her eyes but pulls the seat up to let us both in the back.

Tessa tosses the money onto Erica's lap on the way in. "Money well spent," she says to no one in particular.

As Erica pulls out of the driveway, I catch a glimpse of my dad in the front room window. He's holding up his hand, and I wave to him wondering if he has any suspicion about the plans Chelsea and I have tonight.

****

We arrive at Tessa's, and her dad's bent over, pulling weeds while Janet sits on their front porch in a sunhat, with a glass of iced tea next to her. I think it's cute that Janet wants to hang wherever Lonnie is, even after almost twenty years of marriage.

Lonnie looks up. "Can you girls please walk on the sidewalk instead of my lawn?"

"Well, 'hi' to you too, Dad." Tessa continues

dragging her feet through the grass.

I try to lighten my steps as if I'm walking over hot coals barefoot.

He looks at her and goes back to pulling weeds.

Janet glances up from her book. "You girls have fun plans tonight?"

Turning her dirty look away from her dad, Tessa says, "Well, Janet, we're going to hang out with some friends from school if that's okay with you.

Janet nods approvingly, but then frowns.

"Don't talk to your mother like that," Lonnie says. He's still bent over inspecting his yard as if Better Homes and Gardens magazine could show up any minute for a photo shoot.

"I only called her by her real name. What's the major issue here?"

"It clearly upsets your mother." Lonnie is standing with his hands on his hips, and you can tell he just wants to go back to his lawn. Being a part of this family tension makes me want to run inside the house, but I just stand there awkwardly inspecting my nails, waiting for Tessa to stop acting like an asshole.

"Whoa, I'm not being, like, serious, *geez*."

I don't get why Tessa feels the need to act this way. Why would you upset Janet? She's the best mom ever.

Janet lets out a deep sigh and goes back to her book.

Tessa makes a big show of pretending to be annoyed by her parents by letting out a sigh louder than Janet's and stomping into the house. If I ever called my dad by his real name like Tessa just did to her mom, I'd no longer be amongst the living. I don't even call my mom by her real name. I don't call her anything at all actually.

To kill time once we're done getting ready, we smoke a cigarette while hanging out Tessa's bedroom window. All I can think about is Jason. We've spent a lot of time on the phone lately, but it's not the same as seeing him.

We wait for Tessa's parents to go out on the deck for their evening drink and then creep out the front and haul ass to the pool to meet the guys.

## Chapter Seven

I'm surprised to see Lindsey's car, instead of Riley's, parked under a big sugar maple that has bright orange leaves hanging off it. The leaves are on their way out for another season and for some reason the fall foliage has a calming effect on me.

"Hey, you two," Lindsey hollers out her window. "They sent me to pick you up. I made Jason and Riley pay me, even though I'd have done it for free." She motions for us to get in.

Tessa climbs in the back, and I slide into the front seat.

"Thanks for picking us up," I say, instantly feeling excited for the night now that we're with Lindsey.

"I'd wait to thank me until you know where I'm taking you."

Oh, God. Now what? I look at her to see if she's joking.

"Please tell me you're totally taking us to Paul's party?" Tessa chimes in from the back.

"Yep."

"Wait, what? Who's Paul?" I ask.

Tessa leans forward in between me and Lindsey and says, "He goes to our school and has, like, a huge ass house. I've never been to one of his parties, but I hear about them all the time."

"Actually, Paul's a spoiled rich brat who has parties almost every weekend while his parents travel to God knows where," Lindsey says.

I can tell by Lindsey's unenergetic tone that she thinks these parties are annoying, while Tessa thinks we hit the jackpot.

"Kenny was going to come get you, but I shut

that down the minute he started taking shots with some other idiots at the party."

"Thanks." I give her a grateful smile. Kenny's not my favorite person, and I'd rather not deal with him.

**\*\*\*\***

I've never been to the part of town Lindsey's taking us. The houses are mansions over here. "You weren't kidding, these people are loaded," I say.

A circle driveway up ahead is filled with dented, older cars that you can tell are driven by teenagers who don't live in this neighborhood. There are kids out front smoking, and they look as out of place as a mouse dining with cats. The lawn has grand statues of cement lions and green hedges trimmed into spiral shapes I didn't know hedges could go in.

"This is going to be totally awesome," Tessa says.

"Or it's going to be lame," Lindsey says back.

When I get out of the car, I suddenly feel extremely self-conscience. I have to walk in there, and I don't know anyone at all.

Tessa practically leaps out of the car. She pauses to wait for me as I look back at Lindsey.

"Are you coming?" I'm still holding the door open.

"Please, and deal with these girls who think they're amazing as hell even though they're just as poor as we are? No thanks." She's smiling, but I can tell she's over all the drama with Kenny.

"Bummer, I was hoping you were staying."

"Well, I'm sure Jason will hog you all to himself tonight anyway," she jokes.

I give her a weak smile and say goodbye, wondering how the hell we're getting back to Tessa's tonight.

"Hurry up." Tessa pulls my arm toward the house.

Relief floods over me when I see Jason walk out the front door.

With a huge grin on his face, he strides up to me, pulling me into a hug.

"I thought you'd never get here." He plants a kiss right on my lips.

"Well, here I am." I glance around, looking for Tessa, but she must've gone to find Riley.

"I don't plan to let you out of my sight all night." He gives me another kiss.

I'm sure he can tell I'm nervous by the way I'm scanning the lawn.

I'm stunned by how beautiful the house is as we make our way inside. The closest thing I've seen to a house like this is Mr. Drummond's house on *Different Strokes*. I used to love watching that show and daydreaming about being adopted by a rich business man. I guess I didn't know people lived like this in real life—at least not anyone I'd ever known.

When I walk in the house a waterfall greets us in the entry. "Holy waterfall! There's a waterfall in this house," I say to Jason, unable to take my eyes off of it.

"Pretty bitchin, huh?"

Jason leads me down a long, grand stairway where loud music is blasting. In the basement there are groups of kids scattered everywhere. Some are crowded around a pinball machine set up against the far wall and others are sitting in a circle, playing some sort of drinking game. Through a wall of glass windows, I can see a pool is filled with even more kids. His pool must be heated. Rich people go all out. *How many people are at this party, and which one is Paul?*

Jason pulls me in the direction of a huge wet bar.

It has shelves lining the wall behind it. They glisten with bottles of various alcohols laid out in a neat row. There's a keg of beer, and several guys are pumping the beer into cups.

Jason grabs two cups off the bar and fills them up at the keg, while I lean against the red, leather lining of the bar. He's talking to a guy and nodding toward me. The guy looks over at me and gives me the once-over, smiling at Jason.

"Let's go out by the pool where we can hear each other." Jason hands me a cup and leads the way.

It's like a Midwestern paradise with beautiful orange and bright pink leafed trees surrounding the outer perimeter of the back yard. The pool has a volleyball net set up in the middle, and there's a game going. It's like this is a resort and not some kid's house.

We find a couple of comfy pool loungers off by themselves to sit in. I kick off my purple Vans and sit back on one of the chairs. Taking a sip of my beer, I exhale. "Now, I could get used to this life," I say.

"Me too. I bet Paul's parents don't appreciate it like we do."

"Which one's Paul?"

Jason points to a guy sitting on the edge of the pool talking to a couple of girls. He has his shirt off even though it's not at all hot out, and he's super tan. He has blond hair, and he's wearing black sunglasses like an actor on *Miami Vice*.

"He looks like he comes from money. What is it about rich people looking like they have it all even when they're only sitting in swimming trunks?" I say.

"Hey, don't be getting any ideas." Jason leans forward and cocks his head sideways at me with a half joking, half serious look on his face.

"Hello, McFly, I didn't say he's gorgeous or

anything. He just looks rich." I laugh at him.

"Well, I better keep you closer. Scoot over. I'm damn sure not going to sit this far from you while you're over there eyeing Paul." He gets up and moves toward me.

"I'm not eyeing anyone but you." I grin at him.

I lean forward so he can climb in behind me, and I settle in between his legs. We drink our beers as we take in the scene, enjoying being close.

"So, how's it going at your school this year?" I say as he strokes my hair.

"School's not my thing. It's just okay."

"What don't you like about school?"

"I hate sitting there, hour after hour, while some teacher drones on about stuff I don't care about."

I can tell he genuinely means what he's saying and it bums me out.

"You're looking at it all wrong. My view on school is that I'm being filled with new information every day, and information is powerful."

He laughs, and I turn around and look back at him. At first, I think I might get mad, but then I sit up straight with an air of confidence about me.

"Well fine, be miserable all day, but I'm going to be the first woman president and you won't be laughing then."

"Okay, okay, President Sunshine, don't get crazy. I'll be your chauffer, and I can watch you rule the world every day."

"You can be anything you want to be, but you can't screw off at school." I poke him playfully in the chest and lean in for a kiss.

"Well, we're not in school right now, so let's light this sucker up." He pulls a joint out of his pocket.

I spot Tessa and Riley coming out of the house,

and I wave her over.

"Perfect timing," Riley says as he spots the joint.

We take turns passing the joint and Tessa points out some of the kids in the pool that she remembers from our old neighborhood. I wonder how they know Paul, but then I think that I'm here and I don't know him at all.

The pot catches up to me, and I let myself enjoy the moment.

Paul gets up from the crowd of girls surrounding him and walks toward us.

"What's up, Jason?" He's talking to Jason, but he's looking at me. "I see you finally brought your girlfriend out of hiding."

"I told you she's real. I don't need any of you fools trying to snatch her up." Jason hugs me tightly from behind.

As they talk, I can't stop thinking about the fact that he tells people I'm his girlfriend. My heart soars just knowing that Jason Evans is my boyfriend. I smile to myself at the very idea of it.

Tessa's next to me swaying to the music and she gives me a spirited grin.

I stick my tongue out at her and she sticks hers out back at me. This, of course, makes us laugh.

"Oh no, when these two get started, it goes on and on," Riley says, looking at Paul.

"Well, if you didn't get them stoned that wouldn't happen." Paul winks at me, and holds my gaze for a second. What high school guy winks? That makes me laugh harder, sending Tessa into a fit, and she doesn't even have a clue what I'm laughing about.

"You guys visit the hot tub yet?" Paul asks Jason.

"Not yet, but now that you mention it, I'm going to."

I'm still trying to regain control of myself when

Jason pulls me up to stand next to him.

"We need to separate you two." He's looking at Tessa, who's still cracking up.

Giving Tessa a playful wave goodbye, I head back into the house, weaving my way through the sea of people that has grown since earlier. I'm taken aback at how amazing the hot tub room is. The hot tub itself is in the middle of the room surrounded by giant, white fur pillows. Blue lights in the hot tub provide the only light in the room, creating the illusion of a waterfall on the ceiling. One wall is a giant mirror and the rest of the walls are covered in bizarre paintings—the kinds of paintings that rich people decorate with. My home's decor style is early American yard sale motif, this one is more *Lifestyles of the Rich and Famous.*

There's nobody else in the room, and Jason turns around and locks the door.

"I don't have my suit with me." I run my hand along the front of my stomach, wondering if he's wanting to actually get in the hot tub.

"Who needs a suit? You have a bra and undies on, don't you? It's the same thing as a bathing suit, if you think about it," he says.

"Undies?" I smile at him.

"Well, what do you call them?"

"Hmm, undies I guess?"

We both find this funny. He pulls his shirt off over his head. I'm super nervous, but tell myself that he's right. My bathing suit doesn't cover much more of me than my bra and underwear do—but it still feels different.

As I pull my shirt off, I can feel his eyes on me.

He slides his jeans down, and I can barely take my eyes off his stomach and the small cut of muscles just above his hipbones. He's wearing black boxers, and he looks perfect in them. I slip my shorts off, and he instantly comes over to me, taking me in with his eyes, and my face grows hot.

"You're beautiful," he says.

I don't say anything back, and he leads me to the hot tub.

He climbs in first, and his face crinkles up.

"Hot?"

"Very." He lets out a heavy breath.

I move up the tiny staircase and sit on the edge. I put my toes in to test it. "Whoa, this is hot."

"Get in, you'll get used to it."

"I will. I just need a minute to get my feet used to it first." I look around and think about how surreal it is that one minute I'm at home feeding Zachary cereal with water, for God's sake, and the next I'm in a mansion with my new boyfriend, taking a dip in a hot tub.

Jason wades over to me and places his body between my legs. I bend my head down and kiss him long and soft as he slips me slowly into the water with him. Wrapping my legs around him, he sits down deeper into the water. It takes my breath away as the heat creeps up my back, but it feels good having him hold me with the water rushing in around us.

We continue kissing, and I can feel him getting hard underneath me.

"I've been wanting to tell you something," he whispers against my lips.

"What is it?" I'm breathless against his mouth, still trying to adjust to the heat.

"I think I'm falling for you, and I'm hoping you'll be my girlfriend."

I'm taken off guard by his words. Chelsea says that if you date a guy, at some point he will have 'the talk' with you. She says it will solidify his intentions to be with you and nobody else, and you can either accept or move on. This must be what she means. I didn't expect it this soon. I felt I was maybe in love with him, but I thought that was just me being crazy. I had no idea he felt the same way.

"Will you be mine?" He draws me against his chest.

"Of course." Trying to hide my shy smile, I look down.

"Good, because I already told everyone you are. I knew the night I met you at Lori's that you weren't like the girls I go to school with. You care about school and your family, and I love that about you."

"One little problem." I straighten up and look at him intently now. "My dad is an anti-boy kind of dad. I'm not allowed to date, like at all." I'm worried this will make him take back what he just said.

"We'll have to be creative with our relationship. We've been able to do it so far," he says, placing a small kiss on my lips.

I'm relieved that this isn't going to push him away. I wrap my arms around his neck, and he kisses me lightly at first and then stronger with more passion. He slips his hand around my waist and with the other hand he moves my underwear to the side.

"Wait," I whisper.

"What is it?" He pulls back to look me right in the eyes.

"Umm ... we don't have a condom ... again."

"Do we need one?" He raises his eyebrows in a question. "What I'm saying is, we don't have to go that far if you're not ready."

I pause for a moment, looking around the room and then back at him. "I think I'm ready, but we need protection obviously." I can't believe I'm going to actually do it.

"Okay, well, stay here and I'll go get a condom. I'm sure Paul has plenty because he thinks he's king of the ladies." He slides me off his lap and starts climbing out of the hot tub.

"Hold on." I grab his hand to pull him back to me as panic arises.

"Change your mind?" He kisses me sweetly on the cheek.

"No, but I feel weird about you asking for a condom. Then everyone will know what we're doing in here." I hope he understands the way this would make a girl feel.

"We can do it in the hot tub. I heard that you can't get pregnant in water."

"Really?"

"I think so, yeah."

All I can do at this point is trust him. He's older than me and knows more than I do about this stuff—and I don't want to seem dumb about it.

He pulls me closer to his chest once more. We start kissing, and I move on top of his lap again. He gently draws my underwear to the side again, and I have the sensation of the top of his penis inside me. I wonder when he even took his boxers off or if they are still on somehow. There's a small pinch and a burning slowly grows inside me, but I know he's trying to be as tender as possible.

Chelsea said this would hurt the first time, but it doesn't hurt that bad.

My mind wanders while he slides me up and down, and I can't stop watching the door for someone to burst in. I didn't think I would be so distracted during the actual act, but I am. Turning my attention back to Jason, I smile and relax.

He whispers that he loves me and lets out a long, slow moan as he slows and I'm surprised that it's over.

Kissing his neck, I work my way around to his mouth. Looking into his eyes, I grin.

"Are you sure this is your first time, because that was incredible," he murmurs breathlessly.

Smiling at him, I kiss him again.

"I love you, Megan Shine."

"I love you, too."

\*\*\*\*

Tessa and I are sitting on her bed, discussing what we did at the party tonight. Thankfully, Lindsey came back to get Kenny and gave us a ride home. It turns out Tessa had sex with Riley, too. They had sex in the bathroom in Paul's parent's room. Not sure why her and Riley always end up in a bathroom. Tessa thought it was sleazy to do it in their bed, and I'm thinking that the bathroom would not be my romantic first-time spot.

She said that Riley was majorly impressed that she had a condom in her purse. I explain about not getting pregnant in water, and she says that we needed to ask Chelsea, because she thinks that isn't true—I worry she's right. I swear to her that I will never do it without a condom again.

"You better not or I'll tell Chelsea. You'll have her to deal with and you know you don't want that drama queen on your case." We both feel somehow changed by the night, and we stay up talking and smoking in her bedroom.

"I told you that you moving here would be a new adventure for us," I say as we're falling asleep.

"You weren't shitting. We lost our damn virginity," she says in a sleepy, slow voice.

We fall asleep in a sort of daze.

## Chapter Eight

My dad picked me up at Tessa's the next morning so I could watch Zachary while he went into work. There's been some sort of power outage overnight that's under his zone, and he has to get his crews out there. He doesn't believe in just managing his crews—he likes to be out there working right alongside them.

He always says, "Meggie, people respect you more if you don't have a problem rolling up your sleeves and getting dirty with them, even if it's not your job anymore."

I pack a bag for Zachary, strap him in his stroller, and set out for my grandma's house. Chelsea wasn't home when I got there. I'm dying to find her and talk to her about what I did with Jason. If I stay home all day, I know I'll sit around and stress about the sex and what it meant for me, wondering if I'd made a huge mistake not using protection.

Now that grandma helps Dad out all the time at our house, I don't spend time at her house like I did when my parents were still married. There's no better place in the world than my grandma's house. It's the perfect place to be when you need a comforting distraction—and I need one right now. She always has something cooking on the stove and has the best ice cream in her freezer. Going to grandmas is like going on vacation—not that I've ever been on a vacation.

She keeps stacks of trashy magazines like the *National Enquirer* piled up on her coffee table, and I love to get a bowl of ice cream and dig through them one by one, reading up on the hottest celebrity gossip. Chelsea says it's nothing but bogus stories, but my grandma tells her she can't say that when she doesn't live in Hollywood. My grandma and I love a good gossip.

The nostalgic scent of marinara sauce, mixed with cigarette smoke and those nasty air-freshener cones my grandma likes to keep in every room hits me when I walk into her house. She thinks those things cancel out the cigarette smoke, but it really just makes her house smell like an ashtray that she dumped Pine-Sol on. I find her in the kitchen drinking her coffee, smoking a cigarette, and talking on the phone.

"Bertie, my Meggie just came in," she says into the phone.

"Hi, Bertie," I yell loud enough for Bertie to hear me.

"Bertie says hello back," she says, and places her hand over the phone receiver to whisper to me. "I'll be off in a second."

"No rush, I'm not leaving anytime soon."

She nods and stoops down to give Zachary a kiss before he takes off to the living room.

I leave her at her sturdy wooden table, smiling and chatting away. Chelsea and I used to drape my grandma's bedspread over that table when we were little, making a tent for ourselves. We would drag all kinds of things under there and pretend it was our little home. My grandma would stay sitting there, smoking and talking on the phone with Bertie even with us under her feet.

She's always on the phone with Bertie, her best friend since childhood. Tessa always says that we'll turn out like my grandma and Bertie—best friends through it all. They've seen each other through marriages, the birth of their children, losing spouses in the war, and becoming grandparents. That's how it should be with best friends. Picturing my grandma and Bertie in their younger days, I bet they were as feisty as Tessa and I.

Married at sixteen, my grandma had to get her parents' signature to get married that young. I can't imagine being married at sixteen—that's only a little older than I am now. She gave up school and left her parent's home all for the love of a man who was eighteen and headed into war. After years of fighting overseas, he finally came home to my grandma and died of cancer five years later. My dad and his twin sister were young when he died. My dad doesn't remember much of him.

Her wedding ring still shines on her finger to this day. When you lose the love of your life, I guess there's no need to pretend with someone else. On her nightstand, she keeps a picture of them on their wedding day next to her bible. They look so young and full of hope in that picture, never knowing the heartbreak that was coming for them.

From time to time when we sleep over, she gets her bible out. She'll sit and read us passages as we listen and nod, but Chelsea and I are usually confused. We always say our prayers at grandmas, but that doesn't mean we understand the bible. Usually I pray for my dad, Zachary, Chelsea, and grandma, but on occasion I add Tessa in there. If I'm feeling generous, I will pray blessings for my mom—even though I don't think she deserves them.

My grandma always reminds us that none of us deserve blessings, but Jesus died so we can be forgiven for all the stuff we do that makes us undeserving. Chelsea always sighs and says, "No way had anyone died for our mother." I shrug. I figure if Grandma says that's the way it goes, then that's indeed the way it goes. I hope she's right because I need some serious blessings these days, and I know I don't deserve them.

Zachary looks sleepy as he settles down with the basket of toys my grandma has had since Chelsea and I were young. Sinking into my grandma's old green couch, I pick up her latest gossip magazine. The headline reads

*Did Love Boat Star Richard Kinon Father Three Children with Castmate?*

I'm so absorbed in reading the smut that I don't notice Zachary fall asleep. He's crumpled on the floor, sucking his fingers and hugging a stuffed animal that's seen better days. I lug him up to my grandma's room for a nap. It's like carrying a sack of potatoes he's so limp and heavy. His diaper is a little wet, but I don't want to disturb the sleeplike stupor he's in right now. His naps are the only saving grace for all of our sanity.

When I come back down stairs, two plates are sitting on the coffee table covered in pasta noodles and the sauce I smelled when I came in earlier. My stomach growls like I haven't eaten in years at the sight of the pasta. I can show up here with zero appetite, and when my grandma sets out food, I'm suddenly starving.

"Boy am I glad you showed up. How would I eat all this pasta alone?" Grandma comes moseying in carrying two glasses of iced tea.

"I do what I can to help out," I say, talking around the huge bite I took.

She takes a cigarette out of her cigarette purse. I don't know how she can eat and smoke at the same time, but she does.

"Do you need me to keep Zachary? I think your dad's working this job all night."

I tell her my plan is to hang with her tonight as I continue shoveling the pasta into my mouth.

"You mean you and Tessa aren't going to run around town looking for trouble?"

Tessa's not my grandma's favorite either, but I think she understands that best friends are what they are. I'm surprised to feel tears slide down my cheeks and my throat burn with the sudden onslaught of my emotions. I set my fork down and give in to the cry I know can't be stopped at this point.

She stamps her cigarette out. "What's a matter? Is it Tessa?" I shake my head no. She takes my hand in hers, and I try to get a hold of myself. "I can't help you if you don't talk to me Meggie."

With concern behind her eyes, she patiently waits for me to speak.

"I have a boyfriend," I say.

"And?" She's still holding my hand.

"And, I think I love him. Well, actually I do love him. I know that most people don't think you can fall in love at my age or so fast, but I did and I'm afraid."

"And you're afraid of?" She knows the answer to this question, but I think she's making sure it isn't something more.

"I'm afraid that he won't want to stay with me because dad won't let me date."

"Mmhmm, I thought that was the issue." She sits back on the couch and stares up at the ceiling for a minute, mulling over what to say to me. "You know your dad acts this way because he worries about you girls. I know it seems like he's trying to ruin your life, but he's just concerned for your wellbeing."

"I know, but it's not fair grandma. I love Jason."

"Jason. I like that name. Jason," she says once more.

This makes me smile. "I like it too."

"I know that kind of love, I had it at your very same age with your grandfather. I did every single thing I could to be with him against my parents' wishes. I suppose it turned out okay, because I got all of you in the end. True love can be at any age, I believe that, but that doesn't mean it's easy."

She isn't telling me I can or can't be with Jason. Her understanding is exactly what I needed to hear.

"Just be careful and don't do anything you shouldn't." She winks at me and relites her cigarette. "The TV Guide that just came says they're having two episodes of *The Golden Girls* back-to-back tonight."

"Perfect," I say.

*The Golden Girls* is a new show on TV that my grandma and Bertie are obsessed with. The women on the show seem to be having the time of their lives. I wonder if my grandma secretly wishes her and Bertie could live in a house with Edie and Agnes, their other girlfriends. They could eat cheesecake together in their robes at midnight or play cards on a Saturday afternoon, drinking some fruity rum drink like the Golden Girls.

We are stuffed full of pasta, and my grandma says she's going to lie down on the couch and rest her eyes for a couple minutes. She'll never admit that what she's actually doing is taking a nap. It's like she thinks she's not allowed to have a nap. When I'm her age, I'll take a nap when I damn well please, and not give a hoot what anyone thinks.

I swear, I barely get the dishes started before I already hear her snoring away.

I slip out to the back patio with one of her cigarettes. I'd never smoke in front of her, but I have a feeling she knows I do it anyway. She started at thirteen so maybe she figures who's she to tell me I can't do it. Sitting out here, I can feel winter coming. There's a breeze swirling about that's not quite cold, but by no means warm.

In Missouri, you can be going along having fall at eighty-five degrees and then suddenly, bam, its forty-five degrees, and you're trying to figure out how it happened so fast. That day is coming, I can feel it.

Going back in to grab the phone, I drag it out to the patio with me. My grandma's phone cord is so long that Chelsea always jokes that if we stretched it out, we could reach the Statue of Liberty with it. I call home to see if Chelsea's there yet. I'm losing my mind thinking about the hot-tub situation with Jason. There's no answer.

I hang up and call Erica's house, hoping she's there. Erica's mom says that they went to the mall. I'm going to have to wait until she gets home and try to calm down in the meantime. She's going to have a field day over me having sex without a condom, and it's beginning to freak me out so badly I can't think of anything else. I even debate telling grandma, but I think that would be a little too much for her to deal with.

I try not to concentrate on every minute that ticks by. Letting the sun warm my face in the cool breeze, I tell myself I'm okay. It was my first time, for crying out loud, and Chelsea does it all the time.

The phone rings, startling me awake. I guess I must've dozed off in the chair. I quickly answer it, hoping it doesn't wake my brother or grandma.

"Hello?"

"Meg, is something up? Nobody was here when I got home. Erica's mom said you're looking for me," Chelsea says. Her tone sounds half-annoyed but also a little concerned.

*I had sex, and I'm freaked out.*

"No, nothing major. Dad had to work so I'm hanging out over here with grandma and Zachary. I think we're going to sleep over. *So*, you want to come hang with us?" My voice is shaky, and I know she senses something is going on with me.

She sighs. "Yeah, okay. I'll be over in a little."

"Really?" I'm shocked. Normally she has plans with her boyfriend on a Saturday night. This is also known as, sleeping at Erica's, if you're my dad.

"Yeah, Meg, I said I would." Now sounding drained, she tells me she'll bring extra diapers and see me soon.

The feeling that I'm not alone strikes me, and I turn to see Zachary pressing his mouth to the glass door. Thankfully, he still has his diaper on, though it's drooping with pee like a water balloon being held by the tip.

I change him and heat up some pasta, minus the sauce. No way am I cleaning up a sauce mess right now.

Grandma saunters into the kitchen from her nap searching for her lighter with her hair looking like she just came in from a tornado. That must have been some nap she didn't take. I hand her the lighter, explaining that I didn't want Zachary getting a hold of it.

She looks at me for a long second. "I guess you expect me to believe that's why you have it." I give her a sheepish grin, and she raises her eyebrows in a look that says, "I know you better than you think, so cut the crap."

Zachary is finally finished eating after trying to lodge half his pasta noodles up his nose.

To distract myself, I cart him out front with some toy trucks while we wait for Chelsea.

His squeals alert me the minute Chelsea's on grandma's street. He can see her coming and begins to holler and clap his hands, yelling for her to, "Huwwey, huwwey".

My brother has exhausted himself with all the jumping up and down by the time Chelsea makes it down the street to us.

She gives him a quick kiss on the head and looks at me. "Spill it. I know you did something I told you not to do, and now you're freaked out."

We settle Zachary back down with his trucks, and I tell her exactly what happened.

She waits until I'm done talking and then starts in on me. "First, you're a complete idiot for thinking you can't get pregnant having sex in water. Second, if you're pregnant, Dad will kill you, so you won't have to worry about what to do. Lastly, I'm taking you to my clinic to get you on birth control because I know you're dumb enough to do this again."

She asks me when my last period was, and I start crying. I tell her I'm getting ready to start my period in the next couple of days. She says I'm probably fine because you usually get pregnant a couple days after your period ends.

Staring at her blankly, I'm confused.

"Honestly, Meg, if you're going to have sex, you need to read up on your reproductive cycle, and stop being dumb."

Being called an idiot, stupid, and dumb within five minutes hasn't cheered me up, but I know she's right. I need to call Jason and let him know that we can't be this clueless about sex from now on. I hate when my sister is right.

Later that night, Chelsea and I watch *The Golden Girls* and polish off the rest of the pasta with grandma and Zachary.

Grandma takes Zachary to bed with her, and I tell Chelsea I'm going to go call Jason and tell him what she told me. Usually, she would tell me she wants to use the phone, but since I'm acting like the whole purpose of my call is to inform Jason about how knowledgeable she is and how dumb we are, she allows it without a fight.

She gives me some privacy and goes into the kitchen with a magazine to find some of grandma's wine. Grandma allows Chelsea to drink wine, only at her house and only if she sleeps over. I don't care for wine. I'm more of a beer girl. Chelsea says that's because I'm not mature in my drinking—I think that's dumb.

Jason's phone rings like ten times before his mom finally answers it. She tells me that he and Riley and some other guys are playing darts in the garage. I hear her set the phone down with a loud clank to go get him.

"Damn, Sunshine, it took you long enough to call me. I've been wondering when I'd get to hear your voice."

Happiness swells inside me knowing he was waiting for me to call.

"Well, I've been on Zachary duty."

"I know what you mean. I've been on Kenny duty."

This makes me laugh even though it's sort of sad. I tell him—in a much nicer way than Chelsea told me—everything she said about sex in water and my period. I also inform him that she wants me to get on the pill. He says he's sorry and that Kenny told him about the water. If I'd known he got this advice from his brother, I'd never have believed him at Paul's party.

"Well you know I'm on board with you getting on the pill. I plan to make love to you every chance I get."

This makes my insides vibrate with a mix of anticipation and excitement. We talk for a little longer before Chelsea interrupts us to say she needs to use the phone and she's coming back in five minutes to take it.

"Sounds like the boss needs you to get off."

"Yeah, I have to go."

"Hey, next Friday night is Lindsey's birthday, and Kenny has talked her into going out. Can we come get you?"

"Um, Jason, you can't ever come get me, but I'll see what I can work out."

"You better," he teases.

"I will." I have no clue how I will make it happen.

"Okay. And. Sunshine?"

"Yeah?"

"I love you."

"I love you too," I whisper so Chelsea doesn't hear me, and I hang up.

## Chapter Nine

"I heard you did the deed." Erica turns the radio down as I climb in the backseat of her car after school Monday.

"Great. Who else have you told?" I look back at Chelsea and wonder who all she blabbed to.

"I had to tell Erica, because I had to get you a ride to the clinic, didn't I?"

Chelsea climbs into the front seat, shooting me an annoyed look and rolling her eyes. Chelsea's not wasting time making me get on birth control. Guessing she has a point, I keep my mouth shut. She tells me that the clinic doesn't require parents, but I have to pay cash for an exam and my first month of pills today.

"What? Why are you just now telling me this? I only have twenty bucks to my name and that took forever for me to save as it is. What the hell am I supposed to do?" I realize I have an attitude and say, "I'm sorry, I'm not prepared for all this."

"Well you could've asked your boyfriend, but I guess that thought escaped your unprepared mind." She doesn't even turn around and look at me when she says this.

"Yeah, well I don't get to see my boyfriend like you do."

"That's because you decided to date some guy from Tessa's school. Not a smart move in my opinion."

"Smart move? What's that supposed to mean? Also, he's not some guy. Whatever, can you loan me the money? I'll pay you back when I actually do get to see my boyfriend." Even though Chelsea's acting like a royal jerk right now, I get a small thrill out of saying the words *my boyfriend*.

She says that she has enough to cover the rest, but

I'll have to pay her back, and I'd better figure it out. I suppose I should be more thankful to my sister because she's kind of been the only person looking out for me— even if she treats me like I'm a complete idiot. I might be ignorant about this, but when it comes to other things, I'm way smarter than her and she knows it. She never shows me her report card, and we both know why.

We get to the clinic, and Erica decides to wait in the car. She says she hates going in there for herself, let alone for someone else.

"I don't need the nurses looking at me all judgey. They do it enough when I have an appointment," she says as Chelsea and I get out of her car.

\*\*\*\*

After paying to have an older man violate me in the weirdest legal way, I follow Chelsea out to Erica's car. The exam was so embarrassing that all I could do was nod when the nurse gave me the pills and made me promise to use condoms until the birth control kicked in. Chelsea stops at a trash can in the parking lot, digs the condoms out of her purse, and tosses them in.

"Hey, don't I need those?" I'm shocked that my protection is now laying in a nasty trash barrel with thrown out fast food containers.

"You need to have your boyfriend buy some condoms. If you have to be on the pill, he needs to take some responsibility in this. Besides, it's hard enough to hide the pill packet at home. We don't need dad finding condoms and killing us both," she says.

"Oh, yeah, good point. Thanks for helping me with this, Chels," I say.

"Well, you better not screw this up. You're lucky you didn't end up pregnant."

\*\*\*\*

Grandma eyes us uncertainly when we get home

like she knows we've been up to something out of the norm. As she slips into her wind breaker, she tells us she's meeting Bertie for Bingo, and Zachary has already had dinner. I peek in the living room to see him sucking his fingers and happily watching Tom and Jerry. Dad isn't home yet, and I use this opportunity to call Tessa and tell her about the pill and my exam. She wants to know if Erica will take her, too. I tell her that I doubt it because they're annoyed enough taking me.

Chelsea and I have already bathed Zachary and put him to bed by the time Dad gets home from work. He studies me while he pulls the plate Chelsea had ready for him from the dinner grandma cooked earlier out of the oven. I'm at the kitchen table doing my homework, and Chelsea is in the living room painting her toenails and watching TV, pretending she already did her homework.

"What subject you on?" He sits down with his steaming plate of Salisbury steak buried under a mound of mashed potatoes and a beer. When my grandma brings food to cook, she doesn't skimp on the good stuff.

"English. It's a waste of time. If high school kids don't know by now how to summarize a short story, they should be kicked out." I close my notebook and get up to grab the Scrabble board from the living room side table.

"Your turn," I tell him as I survey my letters, trying to remember what I have. I set it down next to him.

He takes no time in laying down the word ostracize.

"What the hell?" I scrunch up my face in surprise.

"Don't say hell. I know, I've been waiting to lay that one on you for a month." He sits up straight with pride.

"I'll give you ten extra points if you can use the word ostracize in a sentence right now. No thinking about it. Go."

"Tessa will be ostracized from this house if she keeps eating all my damn cookies." He takes a bite of his dinner with a smug smile.

"Don't say damn, and good one," I say.

The phone rings and Chelsea answers it. "It's for you, Meg." Moving to the living room to take the phone from her, she has a frozen smile planted on her face, and I realize that it's Jason. Yelling to my dad that we can continue in a minute, I go to the phone downstairs. I pick it up so Chelsea can hang it up on her end.

"Hola," I say in the cutest way possible.

"Putting freshman Spanish to good use I hear," he says.

"You know it."

"Just hearing your voice makes me want to come through this phone and put my lips on you."

"Just hearing your voice makes me wish you could," I say.

Talking to Jason brings out so many emotions in me. I wonder if I will ever get used to the thrill of talking to him or having him touch me. He's like a drug that supplies my heart with a fix of pure happiness, only this drug doesn't wear off. If my dad once felt this love for my mom—and he must have—then I understand why he's lost his mind over her dating someone else. The thought of Jason being with another girl makes me feel like all the blood has drained from my body. I can't even imagine that kind of hurt, and now that I'm thinking about it, I'm terrified of it.

"I know you can't talk, but I wanted to see if you worked something out for Lindsey's birthday? Lindsey can pick you up after school Friday. She's made us promise to take her out for a real dinner. She told me she wasn't going unless you and I came, too. Besides I owe you an official date," he says.

"Oh, so thanks to Lindsey I finally get an official date out of you?" I tease.

"You can have anything you want out of me, Sunshine."

Looking around, I'm suddenly petrified my dad can hear this conversation.

"Well, for now, I'll take a date."

"I promise, I'll give you that date and much much more."

"Hmm, I wonder what the much more you're referring to is?" I say.

"Oh, you know exactly what it is."

"Yes, I think I do." I'm yearning to see him now even worse than I was an hour ago.

"I hope it's okay that Tessa isn't coming. Kenny was annoyed enough that Lindsey wanted you and I to be there."

"No biggie, I'm sure she has plans with Riley anyway."

We agree to have Lindsey come get me from 7-Eleven at six on Friday night. I'll have to think of something to tell my dad, because there's no way he'll let Lindsey pick me up when he doesn't know her. It's going to be tricky because Tessa won't be there so I can't use her as my scape goat. Dating is going to get complicated for me.

"Meg? Megan?" My dad's calling me from the living room.

Good God, can I have five minutes to myself? It's like his dad radar turned on, and he knows I'm talking to a guy. What would he do if I yelled, "Hang on, I'm talking to my boyfriend and we're planning a date that also includes sex." He would kill me, like dead.

"Oh man, I hear your dad, you better go," Jason

says.

It means a lot to me that Jason understands I can't talk anymore. I think he's definitely a keeper.

"I know. Sorry."

"Don't apologize. It's not your fault that your dad's a control freak."

"This is true," I say.

"Megan?" My dad is still calling my name as if there is some sort of emergency that requires my prompt attention—it's ridiculous. Lord forbid Chelsea try distracting him for me so I can have time to talk to Jason.

"Gotta go, love you." I hang up before my dad decides to pick up the phone in the living room and humiliate me further.

I can hear my dad drilling Chelsea about who I'm talking to as I walk up from the basement. Chelsea tells him it's Tessa and says she sounded upset.

"Did you need me for something?" I ask him.

"I was just wondering if you were coming back up to keep playing." He gestures to the Scrabble board.

*No, you were just acting like a nut case because you didn't know who I was talking to.*

"Oh, I was just trying to calm Tess down," I say, and start chewing on a cuticle, pretending there's nothing going on out of the norm.

"What's wrong over in Tindle paradise?" He's staring right at me with his gaze blazing into my lying face.

Tindle is Tessa's last name. Dad seems to think that because they moved to a better neighborhood and her parents are still married, everything over there is as perfect as peach pie.

"Nothing major, just girl drama. You know how Tessa gets."

His jaw unclenches, and I sit back down to the

Scrabble board, hoping to distract him from the whole questioning thing. I start analyzing my letters. This game has been going on for about two months, and the board is filling up. It's hard to concentrate on the game when I'm irritated that he wouldn't even let me talk on the phone in peace. Plus, I want to go to my room and think about Jason, not sit here with him.

I find a spot to spell the word weed but again think better of it. Even though we have tons of them in our yard, I don't want my dad wondering which weed I'm thinking of. My mind is not thinking straight, and I only manage to spell the word weak. He looks at the word and then looks at me with a pause.

"The word weak is weak compared to the word ostracized." There's another sentence for you Meggie, using my glorious twenty-two-point word."

He's something else, and I can't help but to laugh at him.

"You can bask in this glory old man, because it won't last forever. I should finish my homework though."

He takes his plate to the sink, and he's still grinning when he comes to take the Scrabble board off the table. When he walks away, I just stare at him with a blend of love and hate ruminating inside me. How's that possible?

## Chapter Ten

At school on Friday—when I should've been listening to my math teacher drone on about formulas—I'm putting a plan together for tonight. I'm trying to figure out how I'll be able to go out with Jason for Lindsey's birthday without my dad thinking something's up. I could say I'm going to Tessa's, but then I'd have to ask her to cover for me. Since it's only Lindsey and Kenny taking me and Jason on a double date, I don't want to hurt her feelings. She won't care, but I still feel kind of awkward about not including her.

I decide to tell my dad I'm going to put in some job applications. He's been complaining to me and Chelsea about getting jobs anyway. I hope he doesn't suggest I do it on Saturday during the day instead of Friday night. Disappointing Jason would be the worst.

\*\*\*\*

Zachary is busy emptying grandma's purse all over the living room floor when I get home from school. She's laying down on the couch, and she looks wore out. He looks like he has about ten pieces of her gum stuffed in his mouth.

"I gave up on stopping him," she says.

It's not like her to be lying around when I get home. She's usually getting dinner ready.

"You feeling okay?" I'm a little worried about her.

"I suppose I'm just exhausted. I was up all last night with indigestion from Bertie's pepper-steak casserole, and I'm pooped. Your brother picked today of all days to boycott his nap, and I don't have the energy for it."

I bend down and place a kiss on her soft, overly rouged cheek. "You need to go home and get your butt in bed, and that's an order."

"I need to get something going for dinner." She sits up slowly.

"Oh no you don't. I'm going to order a pizza. Besides, Zachary loves pizza. Don't you, Zach?"

He smiles with gum hanging from his mouth.

She looks at him for a minute, debating what she should do. Then she touches Zachary on his head and wrangles her purse back from his little hands. Her short black hair, courtesy of Clairol in a box, is sticking up in all directions. Helping her put on her windbreaker, I plop her shoes down at her feet.

"You're my favorite, Meggie." She slides her shoes on and slowly starts for the door.

"You say that to all of us."

She turns around giving me a wink, blowing me a kiss as she heads out to her car. That woman is one of a kind. I head to the kitchen to dig through the stack of pizza coupons we keep in one of our many junk drawers.

I order the pizza and grab Zachary, taking him into the bathroom with me so I can shower. We learned the hard way that you can't leave him entertained with a pile of toys while taking a fast shower. He once ate pieces of our Lite Brite and scattered board games all over the house. We found Monopoly money and little Candyland cards all over the place for weeks.

We found out about the Lite Brite pieces, because two little colored pegs showed up in his diaper a couple days later. Dad swears he only left him alone for five minutes, but that turned out to be plenty of time for Zachary to do some damage. Now if we're alone and need a shower, we lock him in the bathroom with us.

I plop him on the bathroom floor with a couple of trucks and get in the shower.

It's a rare occasion that I get to take a shower

with warm water. Chelsea usually takes the longest showers before school, and I get left with mostly-cold water like I'm okay bathing in water the temperature of the creek down the road. I'm in a daze, shampooing my hair and enjoying the warm water when Zachary is suddenly at my feet.

He stripped his diaper off and slid himself right in the tub, with a toy truck in one hand and his socks still on his feet. He looks up at me and says, "Bath Gan," smiling from ear to ear.

What the hell, he needs a bath anyway. As long as I have warm water, I guess I can put up with him in my shower.

After drying myself off and dressing, I towel Zachary off, peeling off his wet socks. The aroma of shampoo and toddler goodness waft up to me, and I kiss his little neck. When I hear the front door rattle, I assume it must be dad.

"Anyone home?" His keys hit the kitchen table with a loud jangle.

Just as I open the bathroom door to let Dad know where we are, Zachary shoots past me and out the door with his little naked butt still not totally dried off. He yells for Dad while he runs down the hall. His dimpled cheeks round the corner, and I hope dad is ready for him.

"He's all yours," I yell.

I'm in my room preoccupied with rushing to put my makeup on. I turn around and see dad standing in my doorway.

"I take it your grandma has plans with Bertie?" I can tell by the way he's slumped in my door frame that he's exhausted.

"Actually, she isn't feeling the best. She was lying down on the couch when I came home. Which reminds me, I ordered pizza for dinner. It should be here any time."

"Are you going someplace?" He's looking around my room, but for what I'm not sure.

"Yeah, remember? I'm going to put in some job applications and then go over to Tessa's after for a while."

My plan was to keep Tessa out of this, but I couldn't think of anything else to say fast enough that he would believe.

He nods at me. "Thanks for ordering dinner and bathing your brother."

"Of course."

He goes to leave, but then turns to tell me that if I'm not sleeping at Tessa's, I need to be home by eleven, and he strolls out. He must've realized he left Zachary unattended because I hear his feet pick up pace as Zachary runs down the hall—the kid is a handful. I make a mental note to call Tessa and let her know to cover for me, which shouldn't be a big deal if I make sure to be home by curfew.

I'm done getting ready, and I holler goodbye as I start out toward 7-Eleven to meet Lindsey. I hurry out before Dad has a chance to get up to say goodbye back. With each puff of air, I can see my breath as I hustle off my street. It's almost Halloween, which can mean two things in Missouri, freezing weather or kids sweating to death in their costumes. It can go either way on a day's notice around here. Today it's freezing.

I'm excited to see Jason, but I hate lying to my dad. It's been almost two weeks since I've seen him again, and it's about to make me crazy. Tessa's parents have started letting her go on dates with Riley because they have no clue that a date for Tessa is a night filled with sex and weed. If my dad catches wind of that, I'm afraid I'll never be allowed to go to Tessa's house again.

I can see Lindsey's car is in the parking lot as I approach 7-Eleven. I just now realize I don't have a birthday present for her. I'm a crap friend and tell myself I have to make it up to her somehow.

"Hey, Sunshine," she says in a drawn-out way, teasing me.

Speeding up to her, I notice she's the only one in the car.

"Happy Birthday," I say as brightly as I can, sliding in the car.

"Well, we will see how happy it is once we get to the guys. They have a surprise planned for us. I'm not sure why we both get a surprise. It's my birthday after all." She playfully nudges my shoulder with hers.

"Hmm, a surprise can be good or very, very bad, depending on who helped them," I say, and we both laugh.

I try to keep my window cracked because her car reeks of Love's Baby Soft. I swear every girl at my school wears that perfume. I can never get away from the powdery fragrance. Lighting one of grandma's cigarettes, I pass it to her and then light myself one. I know we could be good friends. She's like Chelsea because she looks out for me, but she doesn't have all the controlling bitchiness that comes with a sister.

We pull up to Kenny and Jason's house, and I notice that their mom's car is gone and it looks like the lights are off inside. Kenny's truck isn't here either. We look at each other and I shrug.

"I swear, if I spend my birthday waiting on these two to get home, I'm going to be pissed," Lindsey says.

We see a sign with big black lettering taped to the door that says,

**Evans Italian Eatery**
**Your Table Awaits**

The sign is done nicely, and we both look at each other in confusion.

"Wow, this is a surprise." Lindsey is smiling so big I can see all her teeth gleaming off the porch light.

We're even more stunned by what we see when we sweep the front door open. The living room has been converted into an elegant dining room with candles lit all across the room with a table set for four in the center of it. It's covered with a black tablecloth and a vase full of red and white carnations. The votive candles have been strategically placed all the over room, creating shadows over objects that would normally look drab but now look mysteriously elegant.

A basket of bread that looks homemade is waiting for us in the center of the table. We're both still taking in the room when Jason appears from the kitchen wearing black jeans and a purple shirt with the collar flipped up. He knows purple is my favorite color, well mine and Prince. He looks so hot.

"Ladies," he says to us in a professional manner. "Your table awaits."

He clears his throat and pulls out our chairs, motioning for us to sit. Lindsey and I are both in a daze over such a wonderful surprise that we barely notice Jason pour us each a glass of wine. The house smells amazing, and every detail of this surprise is perfect.

"Dinner will be served soon." He turns on his heels and strolls back around the corner to the kitchen.

Lindsey raises an eyebrow at me as she picks up her glass, taking a sip of her wine. We hear pans banging in the kitchen, and we give each other a skeptical look.

"Hey, this wine isn't half bad."

Taking a drink of mine, I nod, even though I'm not sure what good wine tastes like or how Lindsey would know either. She does not strike me as a wine connoisseur.

"I can't believe they did this. They must've been working on this all day."

I know it makes her feel special that Kenny could get it together long enough to do something this nice for her.

Kenny and Jason walk in, each carrying a steaming plate of lasagna. They sit the plates down in front of us and without a word go back to the kitchen. They return with bowls full of salad. They go back and forth until all the food is on the table. Once they sit down, they both lean in for a kiss.

"I'd say this is deserving of a kiss, but don't get any ideas," Lindsey says to Kenny as I lean in to kiss Jason.

Kissing him is like coming home after a long trip away. It's where everything you're familiar with is finally back in your grasp and you can relax.

He squeezes my hand and smiles at me.

I think he feels what I do and that's the best feeling of all. We all want someone who loves us exactly as we love them, not more and not less.

Kenny is pulling out all the stops to get Lindsey back, and tonight is a good one.

"We figured that anyone can take you to dinner for your birthday, but not everyone can cook such a badass meal for you. You deserve it." Kenny beams with pride as he looks around the table at all of us.

I raise my glass of wine in a toast, and Jason raises his, still holding on to my other hand.

"To us," I say.

"To us," they repeat. We all clink our glasses and dig into the meal.

"This is pretty good," Lindsey says between bites.

"Full disclosure—it's a frozen lasagna—but we

did everything else," Kenny says, looking for approval. I still don't like Kenny much, but for tonight I can live in the moment.

Polishing off the delicious meal, we discuss what everyone is going to do for Halloween. Once I was done with trick-or-treating in sixth grade, I gave up on Halloween. I'm sure I will get stuck dragging Zachary house to house this year with my dad. Dad doesn't want to do anything on his own when it comes to my brother.

Kenny gets up from the table and brings in a chocolate sheet cake full of yellow-lit candles. Tears glisten in Lindsey's eyes, and I wonder if this is how they were before the drugs took over their relationship. We start to sing to her, and she timidly waves her hands at us.

"I love the cake, but let's not go as far as to sing."

As she bends down to blow out her candles, Jason's kitchen phone rings.

I follow him so I can get a knife to cut the cake.

Answering the phone, Jason grabs my arm to stop me. "She's right here."

## Chapter Eleven

Jason's eyes are wide and full of panic when he hands me the phone. There's no time to even think about who could be calling his house for me, because I can hear Tessa yelling before I put the phone to my ear. The only words that come spitting out of the receiver are, "Your grandma's in trouble!" and "St. James Hospital!"

Jason hears it too. Everything else is a blur.

"Sanchez, we need you to get us to St. James hospital now!" Jason says, and I'm already at the door.

Lindsey drops the frosting-covered cake candle she's licking as she flies out of her chair.

Kenny's mouth gapes open as he takes in the madness that has now hijacked the elegant birthday dinner he worked so hard for.

I'm jumping up and down on the balls of my feet and shaking out my hands while I wait for all of them to follow me out. "Is she going to be all right?" I'm asking each of them as we pile into Lindsey's car. "Please God, somebody tell me she's going to be all right!"

I'm becoming hysterical with every minute I'm not beside my grandma. By the way Jason has his head lowered, I know that he wants to tell me she's going to be okay, but he knows he can't. He leans forward in the back seat so he can rest his hand on my shoulder while I ride up front rocking back and forth.

It takes us fifteen minutes to get to the hospital, but it seems like an hour, even with Lindsey driving like a maniac, flying right through stop signs. I briefly see Dad's Bronco as she lets me off at the emergency entrance. I sprint in to see Tessa in the waiting area sitting with Riley and Erica, and I slow down to look at her.

"Where is she, Tess? Where is she!"

She points down the hall with watery eyes. She knows this is going to break my heart.

Once I am all alone running down the hall of the hospital, I know my grandma is gone—I can feel it.

Her little body is lying still in the hospital bed when I get there. She looks like she does when she's just resting her eyes on the couch. A nurse is rolling away a cart that has some sort of machine on it, and she gives me a slow, sympathetic nod with her lips pursed as she walks out.

Dad has his head in grandma's lap and Chelsea is holding grandma's hand. Bertie sits with my brother on her lap in the chair beside grandma. Her cheek is resting on Zachary's little head. Chelsea is the only one who looks at me when I come in.

"She's gone," Chelsea says, letting out a sob.

Zachary hides his face in Bertie's chest. He doesn't know why Chelsea's crying, and he doesn't like it.

"Shh Shh." Bertie is shushing and rubbing Zachary's back.

This isn't like in the movies where the sick loved-one waits until you get to them and then you say goodbye.

"It was her heart," dad says but doesn't remove his head from grandma's lap.

I didn't need for dad to tell me that, I already knew it.

We found out later, the indigestion grandma thought she had earlier was the start of the heart attack. Bertie told us that grandma called to tell her she had pain in her chest and felt like she couldn't breathe—but she didn't want to call and worry Dad. My grandma always thought about everyone else, even while dying. Bertie called an ambulance because she was worried grandma wouldn't. She was alive when Bertie met them at the hospital but gone before Dad and Chelsea made it to her.

Knowing she wasn't feeling well, I still let her go home alone so I could go out. I'm upset with myself, and at the same time all that matters is that she isn't here now. I want to tell her one more time that I love her and hear her say one more time that I'm her favorite. Five more minutes with her would let me say what I needed to say, but I lost that opportunity. What's life without my grandma in it? She's the bright spot we all rely on to keep us going.

"I wanted to say goodbye," dad says through tears to nobody in particular. "No. I want to thank her for all she's done for us. I'm so damn thankful for her." He's crying hard now.

"She knew, Jon. She knew how much you appreciated her," Bertie says to dad. She's trying to be strong for us, but her chin is quivering and the tears in her eyes are hard to push away.

I've only seen my dad cry once before today, and it breaks my heart in half to see it again. Despite his hard exterior, he loved the hell out of his mother. Chelsea and I wrap our arms around his back as he sobs. If grandma was here, she'd tell him to knock it off and get on with it. She was never one for sympathy when it came to feeling sorry for yourself.

I believe she was that way to protect her own heart from the hurts she had endured over the years. Pretend the hurt isn't there, and it won't bother you. She was a sweep-it-all-under-the-rug type of lady, and by God, she'd want us to get it together now. I smile through my tears at the image of her rolling her eyes at us with one hand on her hip, smoking a cigarette.

Dad finally turns to us, wiping his eyes. "Well, we can't stay here all night, and I'm sure grandma would be annoyed that we've been here as long as we have. Let's get your brother and go get some sleep."

I look around for Zachary, but Bertie must've taken him to the waiting room.

I look back at grandma's room as we walk out. Just as I'm about to turn the corner, two hospital employees go into her room. I hang back for a second, watching the men as they come back out wheeling my grandma, who is now covered in a sheet.

Following behind them, down three hallways, I walk with them as they push my grandma away. They reach a double door and stop. They look back at me, and I stand there staring, unable to fathom that they're going to wheel her away forever. Do they know how great she was? Do they know she's not just another dead body? I want them to know, and I want to scream the hospital down until everyone knows that Loretta Rose Shine was the best of the best.

One of the men opens the double door.

*Don't fucking take her!*

"Wait," I say, so softly one of them leans in closer to hear me better.

I move past them and pull the sheet away from her face. I place my lips to her forehead. Her cheeks still hold the floral, cinnamon scent of her perfume, and it just about brings me to my knees. One of them puts his hand gently on my shoulder, and I step back and let them slide the sheet back up. The doors shut behind them, and I no longer see my grandma. Running my sleeve across my snot nose, I go back down the hall.

****

We buried grandma three days later on a drizzling, chilly Tuesday morning and life has become hectic for us ever since. We no longer have grandma to watch Zachary when we're at school and Dad's working.

We always knew that grandma saved our butts every day, but we never realized just how much until she was gone. Between trying to sell grandma's house and working, Dad has become a walking zombie.

He informed us today that Chelsea and I are now on Zachary duty when we're not at school. He said he hired a nanny to cover during the day, but Zachary's our responsibility while dad's working. Not sure why the hell my brother is our responsibility when he isn't our kid but okay.

"I wanted to talk to you about the whole Zach thing." I'm sitting on Chelsea's bed in the basement while she lays down staring at her ceiling in full pout mode. She's being such a drama queen about being stuck with him.

"What whole Zach thing? Oh, you mean mom and dad letting us raise their third child? What's there to talk about? We have no choice."

Can she ever just cut the dramatics for once?

"I think we can come up with a schedule so that it's not a total suck fest every day. Like some days you have him and other days I have him. We keep the schedule to ourselves as long as we're both here when dad gets home from work."

She looks at me.

I can't tell if she's thinking about my idea or continuing the pity party.

"Why can't we go back in time and not lose grandma?"

Here we go again.

"Um, because this isn't *Back to the Future*. This is real life, and that isn't an option. Can you please work with me on this?"

"Fine, but I have first dibs on days off." She sits up, reaching up to tighten her ponytail.

I haven't seen Jason for a week, and I'm going to freak out if I don't see him soon. This schedule is the only way, so I have to make it work.

****

As the weeks fly by, we get deeper into winter, and I haven't been able to go without seeing Jason on the days I have my brother. He's been borrowing Kenny's truck and coming to see me after school. I realize if I'm ever caught with him in the house, I will never see him again, but knowing he's coming over is the only thing that gets me through the long, cold days of school and back home.

At times, we lay my brother down for a late afternoon nap, and have sex in my bedroom. I have my eyes peeled on the door and my ears open just in case Zachary wakes up. There are days when we lay in bed and talk first. I didn't think I could fall more in love with him, but I do.

"Why do I get the impression that Prince is your go-to man." Jason's laying in my bed, staring up at all my Prince posters.

"Well I can't help that you choose to line your walls with a guy who bites the heads of bats."

"*Oh*, now you're getting personal. Ozzy Osbourne is the king of heavy metal."

I roll over and sit on top of his stomach, straddling him. I'm only wearing my bra and underwear, and he immediately gets excited.

"He may be the king, but Prince is a God. First of all, look at that man's hair." I gesture with a thumb to the poster on the wall behind me. "There's not a man on this Earth that has hair that sexy. Second, the sound of his voice combined with his guitar makes every girl melt."

He yanks me down on top of him and rolls over to position himself between my legs. "Melt, huh? Let me see if I can use something besides a guitar to make you melt."

I squirm away from him. "You better use your legs to haul ass out of here before my dad gets home and kills us both."

He looks over at my alarm clock. "Damn, this sucks big time." He kisses me and gets up, and I pull him down for one last slow kiss.

"You're killing me, Sunshine."

I smile and push him away.

He slides his jeans on and when he reaches for his coat something purple sticks out from the inside.

"Hey, what's that?" I ask, pointing to the inside pocket.

He slides the purple looking scroll out of his coat. "I brought this for you."

As he hands it to me, he holds my gaze. The paper has white doves all over it, and the note inside isn't a note at all. Its song lyrics written in beautiful script. The same script that was written on the sign the night of Lindsey's birthday hanging from his front door. The song is Prince's, I Would Die 4 U.

I look up at him.

"I thought we should have a song, and I know you love Prince, and well I love you."

Tears come to my eyes. No guy has ever done something so thoughtful for me.

"I listened to so many of his songs, and when I heard this one, I thought of you. And no, I didn't but his tape. I borrowed Lindsey's."

"Jason, I love it." I give him a soft kiss on his lips.

The thought that he sat and listened to all my favorite songs just to find the one he wanted to dedicate to me is so sweet.

"I had no idea you had such beautiful handwriting."

"I try." He looks shy and slides his hands into his jean pockets.

"It's amazing and these doves are perfect, like really good. This is what you should be doing. Art, you're freaking awesome at art."

"Thanks," he says.

"I mean it. You have to keep drawing," I say.

"Okay, okay," he says, acting like it's not a big deal, shaking his head, but I know it is.

He glances at the clock. "I'm out of here before your old man shows up."

I give him one last kiss before he turns to go. The snow is falling pretty hard and it creates the illusion that Jason is walking through the static on a television program that has just gone off air for the night. Just watching him walk away makes me long to be back in his arms.

I don't know how long I stand there looking out my front door with one of grandma's blankets wrapped around me before Zachary beckons me. I guess it's back to reality and time to get dinner going so I can feed the little stinker.

On the days when I'm not on Zachary duty, Lindsey comes to pick me up and we go to Jason's house and hang out with Kenny, Jason, Tessa, and Riley. Lindsey seems to be back together with Kenny, but that will be over in a matter of months. She's told me that when she graduates this year, she'll be out of here and off to college.

I want Jason to care about school so bad, and now that I know he has talent, I'm going to push every art class big time. Dreaming of us in college together and how much fun it could be meeting him at an out-of-state university once I graduate is a favorite pastime of mine. Lindsey told me to forget about that coming true because the Evans brothers are clearly not college-bound. I feel like she's right about Kenny, but I'm not giving up on Jason.

## Chapter Twelve

It's almost Christmas, and Chelsea and I decide that instead of putting our tree up, we will have Dad bring grandma's tree over to our house. We figure that it's not going to stay at grandma's house once the house is sold—plus, she keeps it in her basement already decorated. My grandma was a genius. Dad reluctantly agrees. He has to shove it awkwardly into the back of his Bronco, and half the ornaments come off, but we manage to get it all back together once we carry it in the house.

I'm normally super excited to get the house totally decked out for Christmas, but I haven't been feeling well the past couple of days. My back aches and my throat hurts, like I've been eating glass for a week. I'm so miserable that I finally tell Dad I need to go to the doctor. I've been crazily spraying that horrid throat-numbing spray into my mouth—I even tried to gargle it. He tries to give me that nasty aspirin gum from grandma's medicine cabinet, but he finally realizes that I'm like sick, sick.

He arranges for Bertie to take me to the doctor, since he's working. Calling my mother for any kind of parental help is a joke. Bertie picks me up the next morning, which is the start of holiday break from school. I'm super bummed to be sick and not hanging at Tessa's or seeing Jason, but I also feel like hell. Bertie gabs the whole drive to the doctor's office like she drank a whole pitcher of Lipton. Since she no longer has grandma around, I guess she has a lot to get off her chest. I'm heartbroken for Bertie. She loved grandma and lost her, too.

The doctor says I have a bad case of strep throat and tells me I should've seen him sooner. I want to say, "Duh, I know that, but I'm not an adult ass face." He writes me a prescription and tells me that the whole family could come down with it and to watch out for that as if I'm going to go around looking down all their throats on an hourly basis.

I weakly walk out to the car with Bertie, and my fever is raging to the point where I want to crawl to the car. She takes me to fill the prescription and comes to the house to disinfect the sink with Pine-Sol that's so strong it could peel the wallpaper off the walls. I'm grateful to her for helping out. I know she does it for my grandma who's not here to bail us out like she always has.

I call Tessa and tell her that I'm sick and can't come over for a couple days. Feeling puny, I hang up, and my phone immediately rings again.

"Um, hello?"

"Man, am I lucky you answered. I miss the sound of my girl's voice."

"Jason? You sound like an old man."

"I have strep throat. I went to the clinic."

"I have it too!" I grow excited about that for some ridiculous reason.

"Oh, so this is all your fault," he says. He laughs and then clears his throat.

"Well, I'm thinking it could be all your fault."

"If I got it kissing you, then it's worth it. Strep throat or not, I still plan to see you," he says.

We make plans for Lindsey to come pick me up the next day. He says that we can lounge in his bed together all day cuddling, and I couldn't resist the invite even with a fever. With Dad at work and Chelsea having Zachary half the week, I'm free to go. I head for my bed after downing some of the antibiotics I got. I'm zapped, and Bertie agrees to watch my brother for the rest of the day so Chelsea can have some free time, and I can rest. Dad gave the nanny all of Christmas break off so we don't have to pay her when school's out—Chelsea's not happy.

The warm blankets I swiped from grandma's house are piled up around me, and I curl up in my bed. I still catch a whiff of her house on them. Instead of heartbreak, it brings me comfort. Drifting to sleep, my thoughts turn to Christmas. I can't believe it's almost here. My mom's going to miss another one.

**\*\*\*\***

I decide to see how deep Jason's love runs for me. All I have energy for is a hot shower. My natural curls, that are now so long they come past the middle of my back, are slightly tame but not by much, and I don't have a scrap of make-up on. Lindsey says that if he cannot see past my looks, then I should dump him. I admire how blunt Lindsey is, but I would never dump him. Besides, I know Jason loves me despite my sad looking self today.

Jason is lounging on his mattress, hidden under his olive-green comforter, listening to his radio. A blanket hangs over the window to black out the room. He has a little votive candle, left over from Lindsey's birthday, burning on the floor next to his bed. I climb in at once, and he wraps his arms around me. Snuggling into his warm chest feels good, and it's nice to be in bed with him on a cold winter day with no responsibilities waiting for me—at least not until much later.

We lay in bed talking for about an hour when I remember the soup. Bertie made me a yummy chicken noodle soup last night, and I packed it in Tupperware and brought it over for us to share. I wasn't hungry, but I wanted to do something special in return for Jason after the last time I saw him. I read that scroll every night before bed and then tuck it under my mattress.

"I brought us something." I drag myself to

standing. "Don't go anywhere. I'll be right back."

"Oh, don't you worry. I plan to stay right here all day. Strep throat sucks."

As I walk to the kitchen to heat the soup up and find some bowls, Lindsey's laugh comes from Kenny's room and she sounds genuinely happy. It makes me feel good that she's finding peace with Kenny. While the soup is heating up on the stove, I look through all the cabinets and I can't find one clean bowl, so I settle on two coffee mugs. Once the soup is heated through, I pour the piping hot concoction—juicy chicken, veggies, and thick egg noodles—into the mugs. I grab two spoons from Taco Bell, which are actually sporks. The whole spoon combined with a fork thing is the dumbest idea. They don't have any clean silverware either, and I figure his mom must think they don't need clean silverware when she can steal sporks from work. But why the hell don't they have bowls?

I wonder where his mom is. She's always in and out, and I never know when she will be home, but she never cares if I'm over. I could lay in his bed all day and she'd never say a word. It's the weirdest relationship of a mother and son I've ever seen.

"Surprise," I say as I bring the hot mug down for him to take.

He sits up to see what's in it.

"Mmm, smells good." He wraps his hands around the cup and brings it to his face. "You for sure get the best girlfriend award for bringing me soup when you feel just as awful as I do."

We both sip it slowly because our throats still hurt. I can tell the antibiotics are starting to help—at least a little.

"This is the best chicken noodle soup I've ever had, and I'm not just saying that because you made it for me."

Smiling at him, I let him go on thinking I make kick-ass soup. I tell myself to remember to get the recipe from Bertie.

"It's the least I can do after giving you strep throat."

He looks up at me and realizes I'm kidding, leaning in for a kiss.

"How long can you stay?" he asks.

"Well, to be safe I should probably leave at five to have extra time to beat my dad before he gets home."

"Can't you call and say you're sleeping over at Tessa's? Then we could do this all night. I can even make Kenny go get us a movie to rent." He's giving me those golden, pleading eyes.

For a brief minute I wonder if I can pull it off, but then I know better. Just as quickly as I got excited about spending the whole night with Jason, I deflated over the fact that I will never be able to stay here and rent movies with him. It's like being told you won the lottery but then realizing you overlooked one number.

"No, because he didn't want me going to Tessa's today with strep throat," I say.

"Well, then I will just have to enjoy the time I get," he says.

It hits me again how understanding he is about my dad, and I'm lucky to have a guy like him. Most guys wouldn't put up with any of this. Tessa always tells me I'm worth it, and I suppose she's right—at least Jason makes me feel like I am.

We finish our soup, and I take Jason's mug from him, setting them both down on the floor. Warm and satisfied, I'm ready for more cuddling.

He leans in behind me and kisses the back of my neck. Goose bumps trickle down my back. He pulls my shirt off over my head and unhooks my bra.

When I turn to face him, he takes off his shirt, and I press my bare chest to his. He lays me back, and he's already removing his pants, gently maneuvering himself inside of me. As he takes over my body, I know I'm totally in love with him. I didn't plan to love him in a way that scares me, and I'm not sure how to handle that with a dad like mine. In the last month, I've come to depend on Jason to be there, and the thought that one slip up could keep us apart is unthinkable.

****

I wake in pure darkness to Jason's mom calling down the hall to him.

I sit up. "Is that your mom?"

He rolls toward me. "Mmmmhmmm. She just got home from work. You know she doesn't care if you're here."

I lay back down, pulling the comforter up to fight the chills I'm having.

"Holy shit, my mom gets off at six!" Jason turns over so fast it frightens me.

I fly out of bed. "Wait, what? Are you telling me you think it's after six o' clock?"

I quickly move to his window, lift the blanket covering it, and panic. It's dark outside. "Oh my God, oh my God, oh my God. I'm dead. What am I going to do? Where's Lindsey?"

He's already out in the hall running toward Kenny's room. While I'm quickly pulling all my clothes back on, I hear him bang on Kenny's door.

Lindsey comes rushing out.

"Crap! We slept the whole day away!" Lindsay says. She sees me come around the corner and says, "Is your dad going to kill you?"

I don't answer her as I'm moving around like a

hamster on its wheel. It feels like I'm running in circles, gathering my stuff.

I give Jason a fast peck on his lips and hurry out to Lindsey's car darting past Jason's mom. I'm too stressed to say anything to her now that I'm in full panic mode.

Lindsey's still slipping her boots on, and she pauses on the porch to pull them up, trying to hurry.

My dad's probably home and calling everywhere looking for me, since I didn't leave a note when I left. I'd planned to be home before him obviously. I'm not even supposed to be gone at all today, and this is going to be the nightmare I've been dreading all along.

Lindsey gets me home pretty fast, but at this point I'm so screwed I don't know that it matters. We turn the corner to my street, and my dad's Bronco is parked in the driveway. The front door is open, and I can see him through the glass door pacing in the living room like a lion in its cage. I don't get out of the car yet—I'm frozen with fear.

Lindsey looks at me frowning and thinking. "Just say you were at Tessa's. Say we lost track of time and you know you shouldn't have gone out and you're sorry."

I shake my head. "You don't understand, there will be no reasoning with him. When he's pissed an apology just makes him madder." I debate on having her drive me back to Jason's or just away from here. Knowing I have to face this but not wanting to, I take a deep breath.

"Is there anything I can do? I can come in with you?"

"Thanks, but he doesn't know you, and that will make it worse. I'm not going to subject you to this shit." I flip her visor down and look in the tiny mirror. Do I look like I've been having sex burrowed in my boyfriend's bed all day? God I'm screwed."

She squeezes my hand as I get out of her car.

I look up at the front door. Here goes the end to my social life.

## Chapter Thirteen

I'm completely clueless about whether or not my dad called over to Tessa's. I'm an idiot for not calling her to check before I left Jason's house. I have no way of knowing if I can use Tessa as an excuse, and I wonder if he saw me get out of Lindsey's car. All I can do is try to lie and pray for a miracle. I'm shaking as I move up the steps to my front door.

"Where in the hell have you been?" My dad is charging at me like a man on a mission.

I notice Chelsea standing off by the kitchen with a look of fear spread across her face. Whenever my dad gets this pissed, it scares everyone—even if you aren't the one in trouble.

"I … uh … Tessa and I…" Anything I planned to say wasn't coming out correctly.

"Megan, don't you dare continue with the bullshit that's about to come from your lying mouth. I called over to Tessa's, and Janet said she's at the movie with her boyfriend. Her boyfriend! So, I guess Tessa can run around town with guys now, and you think you can hide that from me?"

"I was over at a friend's house."

"I know all your friends, and nobody has seen you. You have about five seconds to tell me who the hell brought you home and from where," he roars at me.

I glance at Chelsea and her eyes say, "Don't you dare tell him the truth."

"I was with a friend who you don't know from Tessa's school. Her name's Lindsey," I say. I mean, I'm pretty much telling the truth. "I lied about Tessa because you don't know Lindsey, and I knew you'd be mad that I was with someone you don't know. Honestly, Dad, what's the big deal? I'm home safe, and she's a girl I have become friends with."

I was doing fine until I added that last part.

"What's the big deal? I'll tell you what the big damn deal is. I don't approve of you riding around in a car with someone I don't know! Not to mention, I had no clue where you were when I got home from work. That's the big deal! You could've been dead in a ditch someplace, and I was worried sick. Unlike your mother, I want to know where my kids are!"

The fact that he threw my mother into this outrages me.

"You know what, Dad, it's not even seven o'clock, so I'm pretty sure me being dead in a ditch is overboard. And leave Mom out of this! I'm sick of hearing how Mom has let you down!" I run for my room before the stunned silence that's currently keeping my dad frozen in place sends him after me. I'm sure Chelsea thinks I've lost my mind talking to him this way.

I sit on my bed like a worm waiting for a bird to swoop in and kill it. At any moment he's going to come storming through my door ready to ground me forever. I wait and wait, but he never does.

It seems like I've been in there all night before I hear him in the next room putting Zachary to bed. The house is quiet, and I crack my door slowly open and see a glow of light beaming from under his bedroom door. He must be in there with his lamp on, probably asleep. He has been going to bed when Zachary goes to bed lately. During winter, it's like we get tired earlier and earlier the longer the cold lasts, and we're in the thick of it.

I tiptoe down to Chelsea's room, being as quiet as I've ever been. She's sitting on her bed skimming through a Seventeen magazine and looks up at me when I come in. I'm guessing she spent the day hanging new posters in her room because her walls are covered in Boy

George. Culture Club's a cool band, but Prince is better. My taste in music has always been better than hers. Grandma would say different doesn't mean someone's better than someone else. It's hard to keep that in mind, especially without her here to remind me.

"You're in deep shit. What in the hell were you thinking going out without leaving a note and then coming back after Dad got home? Thanks for that, by the way, because the whole time he was calling around for you, he was yelling at me."

"You think I did that on purpose? I fell asleep at Jason's."

"I hope it was worth it, because he's not going to let you leave the house any time soon, and you definitely won't be going to Tessa's." I can tell she's sad for me by the absence of anger in her expression, but also annoyed I screwed up this badly.

"Dad can get over it. I'm sick of hearing about how Mom doesn't give a damn, and I'm sick of him being such a control freak."

"Okay. Sure. Good luck with that." She gets up and starts readying herself for bed.

"Are you feeling okay?" I'm used to a longer lecture from her, and she never goes to bed this early.

"No, I have your stupid strep throat, and after today we'll both be on Dad's radar." She leaves to go up to the bathroom, and I go back to my room.

Trying to figure out how I will ever see Jason again, I lay in bed staring at my ceiling. My dad finding out about Janet letting Tessa go out with Riley is not good. Everything is going to be such a mess now. My throat hurts, and I'm still tired, despite sleeping all day. As tears roll down my eyes, all I can think about is getting back to Jason. I don't know how I finally fell asleep.

****

I wake the next morning to Zachary poking me in the eye. "Gan, time get me."

This is his way of repeating whatever Chelsea told him to come say to me. I realize as I sit up that my throat feels better. At least my antibiotic is working—that's something positive for once. I eye Zachary, and he exhales his cracker breath inches from my face. I run my hands across my face, trying to wake up fully.

He gallops around my room with happiness at the prospect of me getting out of bed.

Why can't we all be as happy as my brother in the morning?

He pulls me down the hall, and I wonder whose home. Chelsea's in the kitchen crouched down cleaning up cereal that has been tossed to the floor.

"Is Dad home?" I dart my eyes cautiously around the room.

"Yeah, Meg. He called in sick to work so he can make sure you stay chained to the house," she says. "He's at work, and it's your day with Zach. I feel like death, and I'm going back to bed. Dad told me to let you know that you're not to go anywhere or have anyone over."

"Great, I wonder how long this will last."

"Probably forever after you didn't contain your smart-ass mouth last night."

"Ass, ass, ass," Zachary repeats.

Chelsea and I both tell him, "No, no, no. Bad word."

His smile turns into a frown.

"Real nice, Meg." She gives me a dirty look as if it's my fault and goes off toward her bedroom.

I need something to wake me up for a full day with my brother, who, despite the early hour, is jumping on the couch and laughing like it's the best thing in the world.

"Zachary, come shower with Gan." I hold my arms out to him.

He climbs down and picks up two toy trucks that I assume will now also be taking a shower with me.

After a warm shower, I'm a million times better physically, but mentally my mind has taken a trip to depressionville. I call Tessa and tell her all the drama of the night before. She tells me she knows because she talked to Chelsea last night.

"How long do you think your dad will keep you from going out?" she asks. Tessa's as angry about it as I am. She feels bad that her mom told my dad about Riley, but I assure her it's not her fault—she knows it's not.

"I don't know, but he's not going to keep us apart," I say. But I'm unsure how, exactly, we will get around this.

"Christmas is in two days. Maybe the holidays will be a good distraction and he'll soften up."

"That's all I can hope for, but to be honest I think it's a lost cause for a while or maybe forever. Who the hell knows?"

When I get off the phone, I debate on calling Jason's house. It's still kind of early, and I'm not sure how to tell him I won't be able to see him for a while. I decide I'll wait until Zachary's nap and give my brother some much-needed brother/sister bonding time. I'm really just killing time, hoping to come up with a plan to see Jason even with this grounding.

I don't want to call him and let him down. It's embarrassing to tell your boyfriend you can't date him because you're grounded. The holidays are going to screw things up further because dad's off work a couple more days than usual. No sneaking around this week.

Merry Christmas to me.

The afternoon's exhausting, but my brother loves all the attention. We play cars and trucks, lining them all up in a row throughout the house. We find all the old Play-Doh and build lots of different shapes and creatures that he insists on leaving out for Dad to see later. We create pasta necklaces using the old pasta we have in the back of the pantry. Forcing him to watch Sesame Street so I can clean things up and make his lunch, I'm ready to call Jason.

Lunch that consists of a can of corn chopped up with lunchmeat sends him over the edge. He's practically falling asleep in his high chair. I settle him into bed and go to my room, dragging the phone with me. My heart rate speeds up with anticipation as I dial Jason's number.

The phone rings a couple of times before Jason picks up.

"Hello?"

"Hi," I say. My eyes close so I can take in his voice, blocking out the fact that he's there and I'm here.

"How bad is it?" he asks me.

"Basically, I'm grounded for as long as my dad decides. I'm hoping he lightens up after Christmas, but he's seriously irate."

"I've been worried all night, and every time I picked up my phone to call you, I was afraid I could get you in even more trouble."

"Yeah, that's probably smart."

"I'm sorry," he says.

"Sorry? It's not your fault. It's totally mine."

"No, it isn't. I should've known better than to let us fall asleep."

"You can't blame this on yourself. If it wasn't for my dad and his over the top rules, we wouldn't be dealing with any of this," I say.

"You're right. It's his fault, not ours. He's not going to keep me from my Sunshine. I'll find a way to see you."

"No, seriously, Jason, I might not see you for a couple of weeks. I know it sucks, but I'm going to be monitored like a hawk from now on." Saying this to him brings tears to my eyes.

"I miss you already," he says.

"I miss you too."

We discuss Christmas and what they usually do in his family. Finding out they don't do anything for the holidays, I'm sad I brought it up. He says that obviously Taco Bell will be closed on Christmas, so they would all be home, but they don't usually make a fuss over it.

Christmas is all about making a fuss, and I hate that he has grown up this way. I wish I had a way to make his Christmas better, but this year, mine is looking to be sucky too. Christmas without grandma is going to be like Christmas without Santa—it's unheard of.

I'm pretty sure I could've spent the whole day on the phone with Jason, but I see the shadow of Chelsea sneaking around outside my door. I tell him I have to go, but I promise to call him whenever I can. It's hard to say goodbye knowing we don't have plans to see each other. The nagging thought of him moving on to a girl he can be with is bugging me again, but I tell myself I'm just freaking out and put it out of my mind.

The minute I hang up the phone Chelsea shuffles in wrapped like a cocoon in a blanket, carrying that nasty throat spray with her.

"It's worse the second day, and then it starts to get better as the medicine has a couple of days to work," I say, clearing a spot on my bed for her.

She looks at me, and I can tell it's not only the strep throat causing her mood. Her boyfriend was seen kissing some girl who goes to Tessa and Jason's school at the movie theater last night.

"Hillary Ransic," she blurts out as a tear comes down her face. "What kind of name is Hilary anyway? She sounds like a slut."

Hilary seems like a perfectly good name to me, and just because she kissed a guy at a movie doesn't make her a slut, but I'm not about to say such a thing at a time like this.

In between her ranting and crying, I tell her I think her boyfriend is full of himself and that she can do much better than some pretty-boy who cheats with girls named Hilary—although I do like the name Hilary. It takes me an hour of basically telling her how awesome she is compared to every other girl before she calms down. Pumping her ego as full as a Thanksgiving Day float has made her realize she's better than any girl, especially Hilary Ransic.

"Look at the bright side, at least you're not grounded forever like me," I say.

"Well, I might as well be grounded because I don't have a boyfriend anymore anyway."

I hate to see her this heartbroken because, having Jason, I can't imagine how she feels. Maybe now she'll go to the state university of her dreams instead of sticking around town for some guy. We sit quiet for a minute, and I come up with an idea to get her mind off her heartbreak.

"You know what? I have just the thing to cheer us up."

I know if we stay in my room, she'll cry the rest of the day, and I can't take another minute of it. Coming up with a distraction is the only way to get her off my bed and out of her head. Patting her on the leg, I motion for her to follow me to the kitchen.

She groans, but gets up reluctantly.

I dig out grandma's recipe books from the boxes Dad brought over that we're still unpacking. I decide we will make the Christmas cookies this year. I know it will brighten all of our moods.

Chelsea sits at the table reading off the recipe, taking each step slowly so I don't get the ingredients wrong. We never paid attention when grandma made them because she knew the recipe by heart. By the time I get the dough finished and in the fridge to chill, Zachary wakes up.

"Stay here and I'll go get Zach, and we can let him help us. He'll love it." Taking off grandma's apron, I go to my brother's room.

Chelsea sits at the table and helps Zachary cut the shapes out while I man the oven. He squeals with joy after each shape is cut and ready to bake.

The house lets off the scent of a winter wonderland filled with sugar and holiday happiness by the time Dad gets home. He walks in as I'm whipping up the frosting and smiles brightly when he sees the three of us working on the cookies at the kitchen table. I grin back at him, hoping to start lightening him up, and he drops his smile as if to say that he's still pissed—but then he smiles slightly again. How can you stay mad when you have Christmas cookies waiting for you?

He sets his lunch tote down in the entry and takes a seat at the table with us. There's a flicker of delight lighting up in his eyes with every cookie we finish. Zachary has an issue with licking the spoon every time he dips in for more frosting, but who can blame the kid?

"Well, gang, we should think about dinner soon," dad says after we finish icing the last cookie. "What should we have to eat, Zachary?" He pulls Zachary onto his lap, kissing his sticky cheek.

"Tookies!" Zachary bellows, and we all laugh as he licks the frosting-covered spoon in his hand.

"I think we should do a Flat Burger night since the kitchen is an utter disaster." Dad stands up, sitting my brother down on the floor and fishes his keys out of his pocket. "Everyone want their usual?" We nod, and he heads out.

While dad runs out to pick up dinner, I clean up the kitchen. It's covered in flour and sugar, but it has all been worth it. Chelsea and Zachary go to lounge on the couch so she can wash the frosting out of Zachary's hair with a dish towel. I have to giggle because of the dozens of baked Santas and Christmas trees that have little Zachary bites taken out of them. That kid is going to have a massive diaper problem later.

Overall, the day turned out not so bad. I took Chelsea's mind off her idiot ex-boyfriend, and Dad didn't seem as mad at me—plus, we kept grandma's cookie tradition alive. Why, then, do I have the nagging feeling that something is still not right? I sense a humming in my gut that something is wrong, but I chalk it up to missing Jason. I hope that's all it is—but deep down, I know that it's not.

## Chapter Fourteen

Christmas is depressing, but we trudge through it. Chelsea and I got a radio for Christmas to share. I'm excited because we finally have something of our own to play our tapes on, but I also know that Chelsea will hog the crap out of it, and the radio will end up in her room most of the time.

Zachary got a toy caterpillar that he can ride and bounce around on. He spent the whole day on that thing, and he even ate his dinner sitting on it. I don't know if this bouncy bug toy is such a smart idea, and I think after watching him bounce all over the living room on the bright green thing, knocking everything over, Dad realizes it too.

Last year was the first Christmas that my mom didn't even try to have us over. We assume that's the new norm for her, and we are correct—she didn't call. Lucky for Zachary, he doesn't know any better, but Chelsea and I notice. As long as I live, I will never understand how she could walk away from her family.

Jason once told me it's a problem with her, not us. That's how he deals with his dad's absence. We can tell ourselves that, but what we believe is that it's something about us that's the problem. Over the last year, I learned that you can't actively teach your heart not to hurt. It's something that happens to you and not something you can force upon yourself. You wake up day after day and realize it starts to happen. You recognize that you hurt a little less than you did the day before, and that has nothing to do with anything you did or didn't do—it just happens.

My dad softened up enough to let me have Tessa over on Christmas night. Her family always celebrates on Christmas Eve, and Tessa has always spent the evening of Christmas Day with us. The fact that he has been drinking one beer after another since noon helped my case. He is standoffish with her, and I can tell that it hurts Tessa—but we have to take what we can get.

"Jason wants me to talk to you about New Year's Eve," Tessa says once Chelsea has gone downstairs to listen to our new radio.

The mention of Jason makes me ache to see him. It's only been three days, but I can't stand that we don't get to see each other on Christmas.

"Paul's having like a total blowout party, and we know you can't go so we thought of an idea that makes it so we can all totally be together." She's leaning in talking to me while we sit facing each other on my bed.

"Is your idea a freakin miracle because I'm grounded with a capitol G."

"It's not a miracle, but it's, like, pretty damn good." She's got that sly smile again.

"Let's hear how you're going to save me from my depressing New Year's Eve with Zachary and dad. I mean really, how the hell am I going to convince my dad that I can go anywhere on New Year's Eve?" The mention of Paul having a party is enough to make me feel utter desperation to be with Jason since that's where we first had sex together.

"*Well*, I heard Erica telling Chelsea she's totally having a New Year's Eve party."

"What does that have to do with me?" I'm getting annoyed hearing about all the parties.

"We're thinking we can all go to Paul's first and, like, once things have been going on for a while at Erica's party, we can all come out and slip in over there."

"How is this a great plan when I'm going to be stuck in this dungeon of punishment still?"

"Geez, don't you see? All we have to do is beg

Chelsea to, like, take you to Erica's party with her. She won't care if we all show up later."

I see a light at the end of the dark tunnel of hell I'm in.

"Tess, you're a genius."

"Hey, I'm the Cameron to your Ferris."

"This is true, Tessa Tindle, you definitely are."

"*Ugh*, but now we have to get Chelsea on board to convince my dad somehow," I say.

"First, though, I brought you something." She gets up and roots around in her duffle bag. She brings out a small box wrapped beautifully in gold with a small green, silk bow on top of it.

"Tess, you shouldn't have bought me a present. You know I can't afford to buy you one damn thing."

"I get allowance for basically nothing, the least I can do is use some of that money to buy my best friend in the whole world a present. I also know if you ever got a crumb of allowance, you would totally buy me something too—but honestly your friendship is, like, all I'll ever need."

Tessa doesn't get all sappy on me normally, but I think she knows I'm having a rough go at the holidays this year.

"Well, in that case, let me at that present." I snatch it from her hands and she laughs.

I'm not prepared for how emotional her gift makes me. I open the box and there's a delicate silver bracelet laying inside that has two tiny stones in the middle of it. One stone is a sapphire and the other is an amethyst—they are mine and grandma's birthstones. My eyes water as I take it out and give Tessa the biggest hug I've ever given her, or maybe one of the only hugs I've ever given her.

"This is the most special gift," I say, putting on

the bracelet, fighting back the lump in my throat.

"I know. I'm pretty awesome, huh?" I look at her and snort, because she's one of a kind, just like grandma.

"I swear, I'll never take it off." I hold up my wrist, admiring it.

I've spent most of the day feeling so desperate to talk to Jason. It drives me crazy not knowing how his holiday's going. Thanks to Tessa my spirits have been lifted. I'm ready to sneak some schnapps and load up some cookies from the kitchen for her.

We don't hear any movement as we make our way toward the kitchen. Dad's snores come from Zachary's room, and I peer in. Once my eyes adjust to the dark, I notice the big lump on Zachary's floor is Dad, covered up with the bedspread from his bed.

Chelsea's in the kitchen trying to clean up the jumble of dirty dinner plates and casserole dishes.

"It's Christmas, Chels, don't worry about this mess. We can knock it out in the morning."

She looks at us wearily.

"I think what you need is, like, a little Christmas syrup," Tessa says as she pulls Dad's bottle of peach schnapps from the freezer. Chelsea cannot help but laugh at this.

She turns around and retrieves the last three clean cups from the cupboard. We take our liquor and a Tupperware full of cookies for Tessa, and go to the basement.

Chelsea catches Tessa up on her boyfriend tragedy and asks her if she knows who Hilary is.

"Chelsea thinks Hilary sounds like a slut," I say, rolling my eyes at Tessa.

"Hilary Ransic isn't a slut, but she's been known to not give a shit if a guy has a girlfriend if she likes him."

"I knew it!" Chelsea says, getting riled up. She's starting to get tipsy from the liquor. "You know what? I should show up to your school and beat her ass." Chelsea sits up straight, being totally serious.

"First of all, we're not those trashy girls that show up to fight some girl after school. Second, if you should beat anyone's ass, it should be his not hers. Third, neither of them is worth it, so forget it." I look at Tessa for back-up on this and she nods.

Changing the subject, Tessa says, "Erica told us she's throwing the most bitchin party." Tessa is stuffing one cookie after another in her mouth as she talks.

"It obviously won't be that awesome because Dad called to make sure Erica's parents will be there. I mean, they stay upstairs and we stay downstairs, but still."

Erica's mom wants to be the cool mom, but she also knows in the back of her head that she can't be the type of parent who ignores the fact that all the kids in her basement could be drinking and rubbing all over each other—unlike Jason's mom who's the opposite and Tessa's mom who is oblivious.

"Well, thanks to being grounded I have nothing to do."

It's quiet for a minute. Tessa is staring at me with sympathetic doe eyes, trying to get Chelsea to notice. It makes me want to laugh, but that would ruin our plan.

"I guess I could ask Dad if you can go to Erica's with me and tell him I will keep an eye on you. You're going to have to be as good as gold until then. One slip up, like if he catches you on the phone with Jason, and forget it. At this point he doesn't know you have a boyfriend, and that's how you need to keep it."

"How does that help me be with Tess too?" I ask cautiously, trying not to piss her off.

"I guess what I'm saying is if you can go, then

your friends can come too. Erica won't care. They can come in the basement door once the party starts."

*You fell for our plan completely.*

"Oh my God. Are you serious? You would do that for me?"

"Yes, but I swear to God if you do anything stupid or try to leave Erica's, I will kill you." As she says this to me, Tessa leaps to her feet and knocks Chelsea over, hugging her.

"Thank you, thank you, thank you," Tessa says, laying on top of Chelsea, with her arms wrapped around her.

"Yeah, yeah. Now, get off me you little drunkard," she says as she shoves Tessa off of her.

I'm so excited that I'm not even tired. I tell them that I'm going to go clean up the kitchen so Dad won't wake up to a mess in the morning. In the kitchen, I stack everything that's dirty in the sink to soak and wipe down the counters. I notice that my new bracelet lets off a sparkle when I wipe back and forth vigorously.

It's like having a little piece of grandma with me, I think as I look down at the beautiful, dark-blue sapphire stone. Grandma's birthday is Sept 12th, and I always loved her birthstone as much as mine. I'm a Valentine's Day baby, and I love that my birthstone is such a beautiful purple hue. It must be fate that I love Prince so much because purple has been my go-to color since birth.

Dad told me the day I was born the hospital room was all decked out with big red hearts celebrating the holiday. He and mom could not resist giving me the name Megan Valentine Shine. I think it's super corny, the way it sort of rhymes when you say it. Now that I'm older, I've learned to embrace the uniqueness of it instead of feeling embarrassed whenever anyone asks me what the V in my middle name stands for. It's hard to picture my parents all those years ago in a hospital room surrounded by hanging hearts and cupids and feeling love toward one another, holding their second child between them.

It takes me an hour, but I manage to get the kitchen back to its normal state. Satisfied that Dad will be pleased at this sight when he wakes up for work, I decide it's time for bed. I start for the basement and stop at the phone on the couch. I can't resist picking it up quietly to call Jason's number.

"Hello?"

"Merry Christmas," I whisper.

"Awe, Merry Christmas, Sunshine. I was praying to the Megan and Jason love Gods it was you calling."

"I can't stay on the phone, but I didn't want Christmas to pass without telling you I love you," I say, watching the hall to make sure dad is still in my brother's room.

"I love you too."

"I get to see you on New Year's Eve."

"Really?" he says. His voice goes up and I hear the happiness in him.

"Yeah, talk later. Love you."

"Okay, love you too."

"Bye," I say.

I needed that.

Tessa's laying on the floor in my sister's room, holding her stomach.

"She ate her weight in sugar cookies," Chelsea says, showing me the almost empty Tupperware container.

"Geez, Tess, you do this to yourself every year. When will you learn your lesson?" I'm laughing at her because she's making moaning sounds.

"It's Christmas. How can I pass up these sugar

cookies that you all only have around once a year?"

"I bet if we did have these cookies more than once a year, you'd still do this to yourself."

I help her to her feet and tell Chelsea we're going to go crash. I'm finally tired and counting down the days to New Year's Eve. The next week is going to drag on, but at least I have something to look forward to. It sucks that I have to lie to my dad again. At what point will he let go and trust us to be responsible enough to date? I'm guessing he never will. Even grandma could not calm him down about Chelsea and me dating someday.

Tessa moans as she plops herself into my bed.

"Well, Merry Christmas, you crazy cookie monster," I say as I close my eyes.

"It's so late it's not Christmas anymore, and thank God, because my stomach can't handle anymore Christmas." She turns over, and she's snoring in minutes.

I wonder if Jason is in bed thinking about me, and I want to call him again. I pick up the phone quietly but hear Erica talking to Chelsea and slowly hang up. So much for calling him back. I'm not dumb enough to piss Chelsea off, at least not for the next week anyway.

## Chapter Fifteen

Dad let Tessa stay over a couple more nights. He told her that if he caught her boyfriend or any other boy lurking around here, she'd not be coming back—little did he know what I'd been doing the past several weeks with Jason.

Riley went to stay at his grandparents for the holidays, as is his family tradition, but he would be back on New Year's Eve so we're both kind of bored. It's nice to have Tessa to help pass the time this week because I gave Chelsea the whole week off of Zach-duty so she could hang at Erica's. It's the least I can do after she managed to talk Dad into letting me go to Erica's party.

Jason's stoked about the New Year's Eve plans. He begged me to spend the night at his house, but I told him there's no way in hell Chelsea would go for that. If we pulled a stunt like that, I knew we'd get caught for sure. I hated letting him down. However, I didn't see any way around Dad and his overprotective ways until I left for college.

"What about this sweater?" Tessa interrupts my thoughts, holding a sweater out to me.

She just told me she has a stomachache from all the junk she's eating, and here she is eating more cookies. We're trying to figure out what I should wear to Erica's party. I'm definitely wearing the new pair of acid-washed jeans my aunt bought me for Christmas, but I can't decide on my top.

"Not that one. It's cute, but itchy, and I don't want to be itchy all night."

"Hmm … okay, what about this black shirt? I think it would be totally cute, and I can let you wear some of my bangle bracelets."

I examine the shirt. It's fairly new—from the

beginning of school—and I like the fit of the shoulder pads and the way the shirt falls over my boobs. I'm pretty sure I haven't worn it around Jason yet.

"Okay. Yeah, that'll be cute."

"Thank God. For a minute there, you were totally acting like you're trying to find an outfit for, like, the damn prom or something." She starts hanging my shirts back up.

"Well, I don't have a ton of options, and I haven't seen Jason in forever, and I want to look totally awesome."

"Jason thinks you look totally awesome naked, so I don't think he gives a rat's ass what you're wearing."

I throw a pillow at her. "Oh my God, Tess. You're ridiculous."

I pause for a second. "Did you hear something?"

She looks sideways, and then I hear it again. It's a tapping sound.

"It's coming from your window," she says, raising her eyebrow.

"My window?" I go over and pull my curtains back.

There's Jason standing in the cold evening air, staring right back at me.

My heart lurches in my chest for two reason. First of all, I haven't done my hair or makeup today since I wasn't going anywhere. The second reason is that my dad could come home from work any minute. I lift my window, quickly looking back at Tessa, but she's not in my room anymore. She must be giving us some privacy or gone for more cookies.

"Jason? What are you doing here?" I say, trying not to sound like I'm as freaked out as I feel right now.

"I had to see you. Is your dad home? I didn't see his Bronco, so I took a chance." He presses his hand against the screen, and I put my fingers up to it.

"No, he's not, but I have no clue when he will be," I say.

Looking around and behind Jason so I can see out to the street, I don't see any headlights coming.

"It's freezing out here. Let me in. I'm sure we have a of couple minutes. Enough time for me to give you a kiss at least." He looks up to see how I can remove the screen from my window.

He's so close, and I want to kiss him so bad—but alarm bells are going off in my head like there's a three-alarm fire brewing in my brain.

"You can't. There's no way I can chance getting caught and lose New Year's Eve with you. Actually, if we got caught, I would lose seeing you forever probably."

"What? Come on, Sunshine. I came over to see you." He's trying to convince me so sweetly, and his smile is breaking my heart.

*Please God don't think I suck.*

"I know, but it's not worth it."

"What do you mean it's not worth it?" His forehead wrinkles and his expression is one of disbelief.

"I just mean I can't get caught, okay?" I'm fighting back the waterworks that are threatening to start.

"What's the difference between seeing you now and seeing you on New Year's Eve? It's a risk either way."

He's getting upset with me.

"I know, but coming in the house?" I say.

"Yeah, you know like we used to do until your dad freaked out," he says.

"I know, but..."

"You can't let him run your life," he says, and he's starting to back away from me.

"Look, I'm not you. I can't do whatever I want. I have a dad that cares where I am."

"Oh, so I guess my mom doesn't care."

*She doesn't care.*

"Wait, no, that's not what I meant. I just mean he's over the top. It means so much to me that you came over to see me. I'm sorry, I love you." I'm pleading with him to understand.

"I love you too. I'll just go." He turns away from me.

"Wait … Jason." He's walking away from my window and back to Kenny's truck.

Just like that he's gone. He didn't even turn back to look at me as he left.

"Gan, Gan." Zachary's yelling for me from his room. The last thing I want to do is deal with him. Still staring outside, I take a deep breath before I shut my window and go to get him.

Coming down the hall, Tessa has my brother on her hip. "Meg? Are you crying? What's wrong?" She follows me into my room still carrying Zachary.

"Nack, Gan, nack." Zachary's relentless about his after-nap snack and it's close to dinner, so I know he's hungry. I let him sleep too long—winter is wrecking everything.

"Stay here, and I'll go get him some crackers to tide him over and, like, a toy or something." Tessa knows I'm about to lose it.

I pull my brother onto my lap and give him a cuddle while we wait for Tessa.

"Gan sad?" Zachary says when he sees my tears.

"Yeah, I'm sad, buddy." He puts his hands on my face and rubs my tears away like a windshield wiper trying to clear them off. I know he wants me to stop it. The poor kid has seen so much sadness in his short life already.

Tessa comes back in carrying crackers, a milk cup, and a couple of trucks. "Lookie, lookie what I have for you."

Zachary hops off my lap, and Tessa gets him settled.

She turns her attention to me. "What the hell…" She looks at my brother. "I mean heck, is going on? Where's Jason?"

Telling her about my conversation with Jason, my bawling gets worse. She gets up and comes back in with some toilet paper. God forbid we have actual Kleenex.

"He totally doesn't get it, Meg. He wants to see you so bad, and he doesn't know what you go through over here."

"Yeah, but at what point do I lose him because he's sick of it all?" I blow my nose.

"You won't lose him. He loves you."

"I don't know, Tess. I think he's more than frustrated."

"He's frustrated but only because he wants to be with you," she says.

"I wouldn't blame him if he moved on." I start crying all over again, and Zachary comes back to my lap.

"Okay, we need to get your mind off this, like, now. There's a new way to curl your bangs in Seventeen's new issue this month, and I think we should try it out. Maybe get a new look going for the party."

Ignoring her makeover offer, I say, "My dad's working a power outage, so I'm sure he won't be home until later, but I'm still terrified to let Jason be over here right now."

"Hello, did you hear me? You have to let Jason get over his attitude and stop beating yourself up." She drags out my curling iron, brush, and hair spray.

Tessa's ignoring the fact that the only thing I feel like doing right now is having a major pity party. I let her start the stupid makeover, knowing if I don't humor her, she'll keep insisting. It's kind of frightening when she starts off by spraying hair spray straight onto my curling iron. What the hell is she about to do to my hair?

By the time we have vetoed the new hairstyle because she made me look like a total weirdo, fed Zachary and gave him a bath, Chelsea's home.

"I thought you were staying at Erica's?" I say.

She stops taking her coat off and looks at me. With one arm in and one arm out of her coat, she moves closer to me.

"What the hell are you trying to do with your hair? It looks awful." She touches my bangs and says, "No, this is not okay."

"We were just trying something, geez," Tessa says.

"Well I wouldn't try it again. It makes your face look weird." She's still giving my bangs a dirty look.

"Well, your face makes your face look weird," I say back to her, feeling lame.

"Nice try. Anyway, I came home because Erica's mom's having her clean out the basement to get ready for the party and said if I stayed I would derail Erica's efforts more than help them."

"Oh, well we fed Zachary and I'm getting ready to put him down for bed."

She nods and goes into the kitchen as I go down the hall to put my brother to bed, hoping he'll fall asleep after napping all afternoon.

"We should go outside and share a cigarette. It's not like your dad's home, and your brother's probably already sawing logs after all that lasagna he gobbled up." Tessa's sitting on my bed, digging in her bag.

"I seriously feel like I'm about to die." Picking up the phone, I call Jason's house. No answer. "How can he not even care that I'm sitting here upset?" I say to Tessa.

"He cares. He's just a guy. He's upset too. You know guys don't know how to handle being frustrated."

"So? He's allowed to break my heart by ignoring me?"

"What can I say? Love's a complete bitch. At least he's not, like, someplace making out with Hilary Ransic."

"*Oh my God*! You think he could be out cheating on me?" I'm completely losing my mind now.

"Holy hell! *No!* I'm trying to tell you he's pouting and that he would totally never purposely hurt you."

"Good God, I'm a maniac. Let's go outside."

We bundle up and go out on the back patio. My backyard is a winter wonderland—everything is blanketed in snow. We share a cigarette out in the silent night, huddled together for a minute, and I'm so thankful Tessa's here right now.

"I know the snow's a pain in the ass, like, most of the time, but look how beautiful it is out here. It's a sea of white," Tessa says, blowing smoke into the air.

"Did you slip out and smoke a joint without me knowing about it, because that's such a stoned Tessa thing to say."

"Um, I wish. No, but really."

"Okay, yeah, I'll give it to you. The moon shining down on all the snow makes it look kind of sparkly, like God mixed glitter with it before he sent it down."

"Exactly."

"As much as I'd love to stay out here surrounded by magic glitter snow I'm freezing to death. Let's go back in." I head toward the door.

Once we remove all our layers, we pour a smidge of my dad's schnapps into coffee mugs and go back to my room. The guys on his work crew bought him schnapps for Christmas, giving us an endless supply at the moment.

I flip the watch on Tessa's wrist around so I can see what time it is. She got a new Swatch watch for Christmas, its neon orange and white, and the face is a cool checked pattern. I asked grandma for one for Christmas, but I'm pretty sure she hadn't gone Christmas shopping before she died because we didn't find any presents. I'm glad because it would've made me feel sadder to find presents she'd never have been able to see us open.

"How's it almost eleven already?"

"Well, you've spent the whole night, like, totally in a fog of depression." She looks back at me and then turns to bury her pack of cigarettes back in her bag.

I call Jason's house for the hundredth time, but there's still no answer. Where are they? Not even Kenny and Lindsey are over there.

"Have you talked to Lindsey since Christmas?" I ask Tessa.

"No, but that's because Riley's gone and we haven't had school."

"I bet you miss Riley," I say to her, realizing I've only been thinking of myself all day.

"You have no idea. I'm like dying for him to get back in town."

"I bet he feels the same." I smile at her.

I'm glad we found guys that are best friends—it couldn't be more perfect.

"I think I just need to stop stressing about Jason tonight and give him space to be pissed."

"Exactly. Just, like, let that shit go and enjoy the

party of two we totally have going in your bedroom."

I laugh at her but stop abruptly because I hear music coming from outside. It's playing loud and clear when I lift up my window. Our song *I Would Die 4 U* is blaring down the street. Then it booms from the street behind us before it fades away. I look at Tessa and grin so wide it hurts my cheeks.

"Kenny has a bitchin stereo. That truck might break down half the time, but that stereo is so bad ass," she says.

I nod and she says, "I told you he loved you."

## Chapter Sixteen

By the time Chelsea and I are ready to go over to Erica's party the next night, I'm a wreck with nerves. Through all the anticipation, I didn't think about the fact that I have to hang at a party filled with Chelsea's friends before my friends show up. I've never hung out with any of them, aside from Erica. It's only for an hour, but that's a long time to stand by yourself at a party full of older kids from your school feeling lame.

In the living room, Chelsea and I say goodbye to dad before Erica comes to pick us up. He's sorting through his albums while Zachary—with a sucker hanging from his mouth—bounces around wildly on his giant caterpillar like a cowboy in a rodeo.

Dad loves to get all his albums out and look at the covers while he listens to them. His albums are the one thing he'd never have parted with in the divorce. He told my grandma that my mother could take everything in the house, but she wasn't keeping his albums. My mom seemed to be satisfied with that because that's exactly what she did.

Chelsea says that Dad should've kept it all since he has us kids, but Dad says that's not how divorce works for men, and having us kids full-time was not the plan in the first place. I think my dad moves between being grateful he didn't have to ever part with seeing his kids and being totally resentful that he has no life and my mom does.

"Okay, Dad, Erica's about to be here, and don't forget Meg and I are sleeping over there tonight," Chelsea says, bending down to kiss Zachary.

"I plan to check in with Erica's mom in the morning, so don't pull anything stupid," he says, looking directly at me.

I try not to make eye contact with him and give away the guilt written all over my face right now.

"Happy New Year, Dad. See you in the morning," I say quickly, moving as far from his line of sight as possible.

"Don't go anywhere after you get to Erica's. The weather's calling for sleet, so stay put. I'm sure I'll be asleep by ten. I don't have it in me to stay up until midnight unless I'm required to." We both give him a pathetic smile and go to the front room to watch for Erica.

****

Several cars are parked along the street at Erica's house when we pull up.

"Looks like the party has started," Chelsea says and turns back to look at me. "Don't embarrass me, Meg. Act normal."

She acts like I'm a zoo animal on the loose that will all of a sudden start jumping on furniture or picking my butt or something.

"Give me a break, Chelsea. You don't have to go into asshole sister mode." I narrow my eyes at her as I climb out of the backseat.

"I think you being at this party proves I'm not the asshole here," she says.

"Okay, you guys, that's enough. Let's go in and say hi to my parents and their already-drunk friends, and get down to the party." Erica barely catches herself on the slick driveway, and we all three slide with our arms out ready for a fall toward the house.

Erica's mom and quite-a-few ladies are standing in the kitchen, holding wine glasses, chatting, and laughing at something as we walk in. A group of men in the living room are drinking beer, perched around a table of food listening to oldies rock music.

"Oh, Erica. You're back. Come in here. I want you to meet Kathy from work." Erica's mom waves to me and Chelsea. We both give a wave back as Erica motions for us to head downstairs while she goes into the kitchen to appease her mom.

The scene in the basement is nothing like the party at Paul's house. Erica's basement is unfinished and made up of nothing but concrete flooring and cement walls. There are two old couches and several folding chairs set up. A stereo is sitting on one of the many card tables, along with bowls of chips and plates of cookies laid out. Black lights are screwed into every light slot, making the room so dark you can only tell who people are as you get closer to them. From across the room, you can see the glowing teeth of kids talking and certain parts of clothing that are picked out by the fluorescent lighting.

Everyone has on black and silver New Year's hats, and the black light picks up the silver creating a kind of cool effect. The atmosphere's more fitting for Halloween, not New Year. I'm sure that Erica came up with this idea, hoping the basement would be transformed in to a party setting instead of a drab room where her family stores old picture albums and garage-sale items for next year.

A group of girls standing by the door that leads out to the backyard yell for Chelsea. Following her over there, I recognize some of them from school. They're pouring cups of Purple Passion for each other. I hate the taste of Purple Passion, and the fact that some company decided to make an alcoholic drink in a two-liter bottle is completely stupid.

Some of the girls are holding wine coolers with flavors like Piña-Colada Fizz and Cranberry Crush. It doesn't surprise me that Chelsea's friends drink this trash. I look around to see if there's any beer and notice some guys with a twelve-pack stationed over by the stereo. I wish I had the balls to go ask for one.

For a second, I think I see Lindsey walk in. Wait, that is Lindsey. She's scanning the crowd, and I practically run over to her.

"What are you doing here already?" I look behind her for Tessa or Jason.

"I can't believe I let that piece of shit drag me back into his life for nothing. All I've ever gotten from him is heartbreak."

She's visibly upset. "Who, Kenny? What happened?" I'm dying to ask if she brought Jason, Tessa, and Riley with her, but during a time like this that would be selfish.

"When I got to Paul's, the party was insane. I briefly saw Tessa, Riley, and Jason before I saw Kenny sitting on the bar in Paul's basement kissing a girl that had her legs wrapped around his waist."

"Maybe they were just…"

"I know what you're going to say, but it isn't a misunderstanding. He was totally in to her. His arms were around her waist." She starts crying.

"Oh my God, I'm so sorry. That loser never deserved you in the first place." I'm so mad at Kenny right now.

"I'm done with him and all his bullshit."

"I'm so glad you bailed and came here. You need a drink!"

I don't know what else to say.

"I do. I could use a distraction. Tessa told me to tell you that they'd be coming soon. I have to warn you though the roads are complete crap so it might be a while."

"Yeah, but if I know Tessa, she'll make it happen," I say, disappointed I have to wait to see Jason.

"Which one of these girls is your sister?" She wipes her tears and starts to get herself in a different mood. She's trying to put on a brave face.

As I scan the basement, I spot Chelsea standing on one of the couches with two other girls. They're putting on some sort of dance show to Karma Chameleon. Of course, she's dancing. Boy George is on.

"See the girl over there with long blonde hair dancing like a drunken spaz?" I say to Lindsey, pointing at Chelsea.

She squints, trying to see in the dark, fluorescent-lit basement.

"That's Chelsea." I'm laughing and shaking my head.

We make our way over to Chelsea, and she pauses, looking down at me, confused.

"Is Tessa here already?"

"Um, no. Do you see Tessa?" She's already getting drunk apparently.

"No, I guess not." She thinks this is hysterical, and she's bent over at the knees laughing.

I step back and look at Lindsey. "Chelsea, this is my friend Lindsey. Her boyfriend decided to make out with another girl at the party and so she came over here to get away from him." For some reason, I feel the need to explain this.

Chelsea looks at Lindsey, and after a moment she understands who Lindsey is. I've talked about Lindsey a lot with Chelsea in the last few weeks and have told her about Kenny.

"You've got to be kidding me! What in the hell is wrong with guys!" She's getting loud. "Please tell me this girl's name is Hilary who was kissing your boyfriend, because we're going to go straight back to that party to kick her ass." Chelsea lifts her empty wine cooler to her mouth before realizing it's all gone.

"He's my ex-boyfriend, and I have no idea who the girl was, but she looked like trash," Lindsey says, getting a kick out of how worked up Chelsea is.

"Hell yes she did," Chelsea says, agreeing with Lindsey.

"You know what, Lindsey? We don't need these bastard, cheating guys anyway."

"Hell no, we don't." Lindsey's playing along with my sister.

I laugh out loud and Chelsea nods at me, even though she has no idea why I'm laughing.

"Let's get you girlies some drinks!" Chelsea dances off in pursuit of some of those nasty fruit drinks—I'll have to make do.

"I like her," Lindsey says, watching my sister dig through a cooler by the back door.

"You like her because she's drunk and 'Team Lindsey' right now. Trust me, the minute you do something she thinks is stupid she gets all judgey."

"Well, she can get all judgey because I don't have to live with her. All I have to do is have a drink and enjoy the night," Lindsey says, looking around. "Hey, they're setting up a ping-pong table."

I turn to see who she's talking about.

"I love ping pong," she says. "I've been playing with my dad since I was a little kid, and I'm bad ass at it. Come on, let's go play. I want to beat all those guys over there."

I groan. "Okay, but I have to warn you, these guys are without a doubt going to hit on you all night."

"Perfect." She strides over to the table.

Chelsea brings me two wine coolers. The flavor is Mango Madness. *Yuck*, I think to myself, but I smile at Chelsea. She clinks her wine cooler with mine as she

155

bops off. I guess this Mango Madness crap has lifted her spirits, because I haven't seen her in this good of a mood in weeks.

The guys are all swarming around Lindsey as I walk over to the group gathering around the ping-pong table. Just as I predicted, they're going to be all over her tonight. She can handle it, so I guess I'll roll with it.

"Here you go, one nasty mango muck drink for you, and one for me," I say, handing Lindsey her drink. She holds it up to view the orange liquid inside and shakes her head before taking a long pull from it.

"Here's to a new beginning that doesn't involve Kenny," she says after slamming most of her drink.

After an hour of watching Lindsey beat every guy who challenges her at ping pong, I get tired. I only end up drinking half a wine cooler and feel nauseous from it. While I sit on one of the couches and take in the room, I wonder where Jason is. Waiting for him feels like waiting for my nails to dry when I suddenly have to pee. The longer I wait the more exhausted I get.

****

The disoriented confusion I have waking up to Erica's mom is bizarre. She's yelling down the basement stairs that it's time for the countdown. I cannot believe I fell asleep—and for a couple of hours at that. Wondering if I'm getting sick again, my heart drops when I realize that it's almost midnight and Jason isn't here.

Everyone starts coupling up, and Chelsea runs over to me. She's totally wasted and oblivious to the fact that I've been sleeping the night away on the couch. Everyone starts counting down in unison. Chelsea hugs me and tells me she loves me, and I try not to inhale her awful alcohol breath.

The clock hits midnight and everyone is hollering and jumping up and down. Looking over the room, I see that Lindsey's kissing some guy. Great. She probably went from one jackass to another. Hopefully, this is only a holiday drunk thing. Where the hell is Jason? The depth of my heartbreak over not seeing him has me drowning in sadness right now.

Not long after midnight, Erica's parents come down and take inventory of who's sleeping over and which guys Erica's dad's driving home. They don't allow the guys to sleep over, but they're not blind to the fact that most of us have been drinking. According to Chelsea, Erica's dad is always the one who has to stay sober and drive everyone home.

Erica's mom brings out a bunch of pillows and blankets for the ten or so girls left. I make a bed up for me and Lindsey next to some of the other girls. Chelsea—the princess that she is—has already passed out in Erica's bedroom.

I go in to check on her.

Erica's standing over the drunk mess that is my sister, trying to figure out how to move her so she can sleep in the bed too.

She notices me in the doorway. "If she pukes in my bed, I'll kill her."

"Be my guest."

Lindsey's sitting on a pile of blankets talking to the other girls when I come back to the living room. It makes me feel good that she had a fun time and is bonding with some of them.

Erica's mom is cleaning up the kitchen and comes out to collect some plates that are left on the coffee table.

"Oh, Megan. I didn't see Tessa downstairs. Is she here?"

I look up at her. "Tessa?"

"Yes. She called at around ten thirty looking for

157

you. I told her you were here, and she said to let you know she was coming. I went downstairs to tell you, but you were asleep. Are you feeling okay, sweetie?"

"Uh, yeah. I'm fine. Just tired. No. Tessa isn't here. She must've decided to stay put."

"I bet she did, because we heard the roads are slick with all the sleet coming down." Erica's mom went back to the kitchen, balancing a load of paper plates in each hand.

I look at Lindsey and she's staring at the ceiling in thought. "They must've started to come, but like she said, the roads were bad so they stayed at Paul's or maybe went home. I'm sorry you didn't get to see Jason."

Just then, Erica's dad comes in, stamping his feet on the entryway rug.

Erica's mom peeks out of the kitchen at him. "You get everyone home okay?"

"Yeah, but there's a hell of a wreck being cleaned up out on Booth Road. Every ambulance in town's out there."

My heart lurches, and I look at Lindsey.

Her face says exactly what I'm thinking.

## Chapter Seventeen

Lindsey and I rush into Erica's room to use her phone. Erica isn't asleep yet, but we startle her.

She jumps back into her dresser, knocking over several bottles of perfume when we come barging in.

Even with all that commotion, Chelsea remains passed out.

I dial Jason's number while Lindsey tells her about the wreck her dad saw.

Erica says it could be any number of people out on a holiday night.

Jason's phone keeps ringing and ringing. Hanging up, I dial Tessa's number, and for a brief moment I think about what I'm doing. What would I say to Lonnie or Janet if they picked up the phone and Tessa wasn't home? I hang up. If Tessa was home, she would've answered by now. I call Jason again and there's still no answer. Where is everyone? It's one in the morning for God's sake.

"Do you know anyone who knows Paul's number?" I turn to look at Lindsey desperately.

"Only Kenny and Jason," she says.

I sit there with the receiver to my ear and my fingers looming above the dial pad for a minute—then I hang the phone up.

"Try not to worry. I'm sure everyone's passed out over at Paul's and we will hear from Tessa in the morning," Lindsey says.

Unsure of what she's telling me, I sit there staring at the phone.

"Let's try to get some sleep and when we wake up, we can find out where they ended up." Lindsey stands up and I reluctantly join her.

We tell Erica good night and go back to the living

room.

The lights are out. Some of the girls are whispering to each other, and some are sleeping. We hunker down into our blankets. Laying there, I can't shake the horrible feeling that's settling on my body like a damp cold towel.

"It's going to be fine," Lindsey whispers to me.

In Erica's living room, I pray over and over again. I used to pray all the time with grandma when I'd sleep over at her house. It was pretty much a requirement for staying over there when we were kids. You either prayed with her or got a lesson from her on why prayer was important. Dad never made us pray, and I've never seen him pray. I asked him only once why he didn't pray, and I'll never forget his answer. He told me that God took his father from him when he was only a kid, and he had nothing to say to God after that.

I remember thinking that grandma could've felt the same way about God after her husband died, but she didn't—I never asked her why. Until tonight, I hadn't prayed once since grandma died. Tonight, I prayed that Tessa and Jason were safe, until I finally feel asleep. I made promises to God that I knew I could never keep. I just wanted that wreck not to have been them. Grandma always said, "Don't try to bullshit God. He knows better."

"Meg … Megan." Someone's whispering my name in the dark. It's Chelsea. She's standing over me in the living room.

"What time is it?" I ask her, wondering if she's sick from drinking all that fruity crap.

"It's four in the morning. Come on, get up."

I sigh and kick off the blankets.

"Hurry up. You should wake Lindsey too." When she says this all the hairs on the back of my neck stand at attention. Why would I wake Lindsey if Chelsea's feeling sick?

I jostle Lindsey awake and head for Erica's room without saying a word to her.

In Erica's room, I immediately start to tremble when I see Erica, Chelsea, and both of Erica's parents sitting on the bed. Chelsea looks extremely stressed out.

"Please tell me nothing's wrong." I'm overwhelmed with anxiety, and my heart is beating so fast I feel like I might throw up.

"Dad called. Tessa's been in a bad wreck—the wreck on Booth was her."

As the words come out of her mouth, I start bawling. Erica's mom stands up to hold me, but I shake her off and run for the phone.

Chelsea grabs my hand to pull me back to her attention. "There were three passengers, but that's all we know right now. Dad said when Lonnie called the house, he didn't know who all was in the car yet."

Lindsey's already on the phone dialing. I know she's calling Kenny and Jason's house.

"Are they going to be okay? Please tell me they're all okay?"

Chelsea knew that one of the passengers had to be Jason.

"They're not telling us anything, sweetie. I called the hospital and they won't say," Erica's mom says.

"Go find your shoes and coats. I'm going to take you to the hospital to check on Tessa," Erica's dad says to us.

"Dad said he would come as soon as he could. He has to wait to get ahold of Bertie to watch Zach."

It's four in the morning, and I know Dad would feel awful waking Bertie and with the roads being slick. He'll wait until a decent time to call her.

Quietly, we all go to the garage and climb in Erica's dad's car. Erica's mom stays back at the house, to see everyone who slept over off later in the morning. Chelsea, Lindsey, and I sit in the back. Chelsea takes my hand in hers, and I grab Lindsey's. We just made this horrible drive to the same hospital because of grandma months ago, and it's surreal to be doing it again.

When we pull into the emergency room drop-off, I climb over Chelsea to get out. I don't have the patience to wait on her, and she lets me go.

I'm stopped by the security guard as I tear into the hospital. He asks me where I'm going. I keep saying, Tessa Tindle, over and over. He goes to his desk and makes a phone call. He motions for me to follow him down the hall silently toward her room.

Lonnie's standing outside the hospital room talking in a hushed tone with a nurse when he sees me. Pulling me into a quick hug, he tells me that Tessa's out of surgery. She's sleeping and heavily drugged, but I can see her. He tells me that her face is cut badly, and she doesn't look like herself. He says if I don't think I can see her without losing it right now, then he wants me to wait to see her because he doesn't want me getting Janet all worked up again.

I put on a brave face, swallowing the lump in my throat, and then he nods for me to go in.

Janet's sitting with a hospital blanket over her shoulders beside Tessa's bed. She holds her hand out to me.

I cannot speak—I'm completely stunned when I see Tessa. The right side of her face is swollen so bad that it doesn't even look like her. She has a gash running from her eyebrow down the side of her cheek that looks like someone took a knife and scooped out her skin.

"They told us that once all the swelling goes

down, she'll get plastic surgery to fix her face."

Janet must be reading my mind.

"She has a broken collarbone, broken ribs, and her right arm is broken as well," Janet chokes out.

I move closer to Tessa and get a better look at her face. Her right eye looks like it has been crushed inward. Putting my hand lightly on her forehead, I listen as Janet tells me that they are concerned about her eye, but they can't tell much with all the swelling. I lean in and tell Tessa that I'm here. She's in a drug-induced sleep like Lonnie said, and I'm sure it's good that she stays that way with all the pain I imagine she's in. Janet tells me she had surgery on her right arm. It's broken so bad they had to use a metal plate and pins to put it back together.

"Megan, I need you to come sit down." She pulls the other chair in the room up beside her.

I sit down in a daze without taking my eyes off Tessa. The girl in this bed doesn't look like my best friend.

"Megan?" Janet's trying to get me to focus on what she wants to tell me.

I look at her.

"The two boys in the car were Jason and Riley." She pauses for me to take this in. "I know I should wait for your dad to get here, but I need to tell you before you have to hear it from someone else."

She grabs both my hands and with tears spilling out of her eyes she says the very thing I already knew when Erica's dad told us about the wreck—the thing I knew in my gut all along. "Jason and Riley were both ejected from the car. I'm so sorry, Megan. Both boys lost their life at the scene of the accident."

Just hearing the words *lost their life* seems so unreal to me. Jason lost his life. She's saying Jason and Riley died, and I can't comprehend that. My mind won't take in that information in a way where I can think clearly.

Shaking my head over and over, I get up from my chair and stumble over my own feet. Janet tries to get me to sit back down. I feel as though I might pass out. Running into the little bathroom in the hospital room, I throw up in the toilet, and drop to my knees. I'm crying and throwing up, and the room slips sideways on me like I'm on a sit and spin. Janet tells Lonnie to get a nurse and asks if Chelsea's here. That's the last thing I recall before I pass out.

\*\*\*\*

I wake in the hallway on a mobile bed. Chelsea and Lonnie are talking to a nurse who is taking my blood pressure. Remembering what Janet told me about Jason and Riley, I look at Chelsea and start sobbing.

Chelsea's crying and puts her head in my neck. She's whispering to me, but I can't hear anything over my own sobs. The nurse tries to sit me up and make me drink something.

Drinking down the liquid in one swallow, I curl into a ball and try to catch my breath. Jason—my Jason—is gone. I'm telling myself that he's gone, but I can't believe it. I talked to him this morning, and now he's gone. How is that possible?

The realization that Jason died trying to get to me hits me all of a sudden, and sends me into hysterics all over again. The nurse slips me off the bed and walks me to the family intensive care waiting room. She asks Lonnie to stay with me while she pages the staff psychologist on call. Lonnie tells her that he would call my father and fill him in. Through blurry eyes, I see that Lindsey has her head buried in Erica's lap.

When I come in, she jumps up, running over to me.

"Oh my God, Jason and Riley." She pulls back and looks at me. "What about Tessa? Is she okay?" She wipes her nose on the back of her sleeve.

"She's the toughest person I know, and she's going to pull through this," I say and Lonnie nods at me reassuringly.

Eventually, I pull myself together to go in and sit with Tessa, after the staff psychologist came to calm me down and ask me a bunch of stupid questions about my recent hysterics. What part of, I lost the love of my life, do these people not understand? Of course, I'm distraught. I just want to be with Tessa. I'm not leaving her side right now. Tessa's strong, but I'm terrified that if I leave her, she'll be taken from me too. I can't lose one more person that I love.

Lonnie fields phone calls from family for hours, and I sit with Janet. I'm told that Dad's in the waiting room at one point. They're not allowing Tessa visitors, but Janet insists they let me stay.

A nurse comes in to tell me my dad wants to speak with me. I've been sitting here wondering if Dad will understand my loss. He didn't know I had a boyfriend, and now he's being told my boyfriend has died in a car accident. I'm sure with the news about Tessa, he won't brooch the subject of Jason with me right now. I have no clue what he'll even say to me.

Lonnie tells me I should go home, get something to eat and come back later as I stand to go see my dad.

I inform him that I'm not leaving her until my heart is sure I can. Lonnie looks at Janet, and she sighs and squeezes my hand because she understands.

Dad's sitting in the waiting room with Chelsea. Lindsey and Erica have gone, I guess. With a quick glance at the clock, I'm surprised to see it's already noon. I don't understand why I haven't seen any of Jason or Riley's family. Did they not bring them here after the car wreck? If your loved one dies at the scene of an accident, do you go to a separate place in the hospital for that? I want to know where Jason is at this very minute. I start feeling panicky not knowing.

When he sees me, Dad grabs a bag from the floor and brings it over to me. "I brought you a change of clothes and packed you a peanut-butter-banana sandwich." He looks down at the bag instead of making eye contact with me. "I figure you'll be here all day and thought you would want some comfy clothes and some books too."

He finally looks at me, and I can see anger mixed with pity in his eyes. How can you be mad at someone but also feel bad for them? I'm sure it's making him nuts that he can't question me about Jason. He can ground me and yell at me, but that won't change the fact that I loved Jason and he's never going to be able to do anything about that. I lost Jason. Isn't that punishment enough?

I softly thank him, take the bag, and turn to go. He tells me to keep them updated on Tessa. He goes into the hall with Chelsea, and he shakes Lonnie's hand while murmuring something to him.

Chelsea looks at me and gives me a wave. Her eyes are swollen from crying, and I'm glad that at least someone in my family understands what I'm going through.

In the waiting room bathroom, I change into some sweats, and put my hair in a ponytail. I splash some cold water on my face and look at myself in the mirror. I look like I did the night grandma died—puffy bags under my eyes with red streaks on my face. I'm in disbelief that this is happening.

I decide to get Lonnie and Janet some coffee from the cafeteria before heading back to Tessa's room.

Grandma always told me that coffee can turn a so-so morning into a doable day. They're going through all kinds of emotions with their daughter being hurt, and I can't do anything to take that worry and stress from them.

As I come down the hall, I catch the aroma of cafeteria food, a blend of yeasty rolls, soups, and coffee. The closer I get, the stronger the smell gets, and I'm hit with a wave a nausea. I've been feeling this way off-and-on for a couple of days, and the cafeteria food brings it about again.

My thoughts keep going to Jason as I walk back to Tessa's room. They had to have been in Riley's car, and Tessa must've been in back. I haven't had the courage to ask how the wreck happened, although I'm sure it's on the news by now. I think about Jason's mom and how he was killed a block from her work. How will she ever be able to drive to work again, knowing her son died on that road? I'd thought the hole ripped in my heart when I lost my grandma could not get any bigger, but I was wrong—my heart feels ripped in half now.

\*\*\*\*

Two days of sitting beside Tessa was a blur for me. I'm due back at school tomorrow, but I want to be here when Tessa is able to be awake and find out about Riley—she'll be devastated. I'm not sure she'll have the strength for any more bad news.

Lindsey called the hospital and left a message for me to call her. I dig out some change from my bag and go to find a payphone so I can talk in private. I'm exhausted from the lack of sleep, and sitting in the same chair hour after hour has made my feet feel like they have cement blocks tied to them. It's a struggle just to walk down the hall.

Lindsey fills me in on what she's found out about

the night of the wreck. I know she had to drop her pride and talk to Kenny since he'd lost his brother and probably knew the details of what happened, and I'm thankful for that.

I have to remember that Lindsey lost Jason too. Kenny told her that Jason insisted on coming to see me, and Riley was able to talk him out of it because the roads were slick. Kenny said Tessa wouldn't give up, and Riley finally agreed to drive them to Erica's at about ten thirty. From what the police told Jason's mom, Riley was coming down Booth Street too fast and lost control of the car on a patch of ice. The car flipped over and struck a tree.

I cringe and try not to picture Jason being violently ejected from a car that flipped over. How could this have happened to them? I'm angry, and now I understand why Dad refuses to pray. Looking up at the hospital ceiling, I don't understand why my prayers never seem to count.

I needed to work this out with grandma, but she's gone too—although I know what grandma would tell me. If I told her that I was mad at God, she'd tell me to look at all the things I did have that nobody else had. I need to be thankful for what I have today, not what I lost yesterday. And she would tell me everything I lost wouldn't matter once I got to heaven. We're only on this Earth for a small time, but we are in heaven forever if we believe that God will be there waiting for us. If grandma's right about all that, maybe she has met Jason by now. That makes me smile for the first time in days.

## Chapter Eighteen

A full week after the accident, Tessa was finally taken out of her medical coma. I wasn't there when she woke up because of school being back in session after holiday break. Dad took me to the hospital after. He hasn't mentioned Jason or Riley, and I'm pissed off but also relieved. On the one hand, I don't want to explain that I had a boyfriend and hid it from him. On the other hand, I'm livid that he doesn't seem to care that I lost someone I obviously loved. He has seen the sadness I've been dealing with, and he hasn't even asked why.

My parents' divorce has hardened my dad's heart when it comes to love and relationships. We've barely spoken to each other since the accident. I thought parents were supposed to care when their kid is going through something—no matter what. More and more, I find myself realizing that my parents are completely clueless. Both my parents have one main job as a parent, to love their kids unconditionally. They're both failing.

By the time I make it to Tessa, she's heard the news about Riley. I can't imagine the trauma this is causing her since she was with them when it happened. Lonnie warns me before I go into her room that she still looks bad—maybe even worse than when I saw her last. Walking into her room, I try not to react at how beaten up her face still looks.

She holds her one mobile hand out, beckoning me to her.

I run to her and carefully embrace her. I'm afraid that I'm hurting her, but she clings to me. I look her in the eyes for signs of the old Tessa.

"You get the award for worst week ever," I say through tears.

We used to try to one-up each other on Friday

nights about how bad of a week we had. Her bad weeks always involved her parents annoying her and homework, and mine always involved Zachary-duty and Chelsea drama.

She briefly starts to laugh, but it causes her too much pain to smile so she stops. "You didn't think I would leave you to deal with Chelsea's drama alone, did you?"

Letting out a huge sigh of relief, I hug her again. This crazy best friend of mine has turned me into a hugger. Damn her.

"I'll give you girls some privacy." Standing up, Janet touches both our shoulders, and walks out. She looks like she's aged ten years in a week. The happy-go-lucky bop to her step has disappeared.

"I've been waiting for you to get here to do something that I know I totally can't do without you."

Sitting back in the hospital chair, I wipe away my tears with my fingertips, wondering what she could be talking about.

She tries to sit up a little straighter in her hospital bed and winces. Her whole right side is basically a mess from the waist up. Her right arm is in a full cast and her collarbone is broken. Lonnie told me she did in fact have some broken ribs as well.

"I need to see my face." I swallow hard and look at her. "I told my mom I'm not going to look, but I want to. I don't want to see the damage with anyone else. I need to be able to react without my mom here. She's been through enough, and I can tell by the way she looks at me that I look like a total train wreck."

I nod. I'm not going to sugarcoat how she looks or bullshit her. I want her to see for herself, and we'll go from there.

"There's a mirror in my mom's duffle bag." She

looks toward the floor.

I lean down to dig out the mirror and start to hand it to Tessa, before I pull it back against my chest. "First, I want you to keep in mind that you're going to see a plastic surgeon, and once the swelling goes down, they're going to fix this. Okay? This is not your forever face. Got it?"

She nods to appease me, and I give her the mirror.

She takes a deep inhale and holds it up so she can see her reflection. She stares for a long time without saying a word, but her silence says it all.

I'm holding my breath.

"I'm a fucking beast. I'm a lopsided fucking monster. I look like I've been hit on the right side of my face with a shovel."

She starts to cry then, and when I get up to hug her, she tries to push me away with only one good arm.

"How will they fix this?" She holds the mirror back up to her face. "How the hell can anyone fix this mess?" She's getting hysterical, and she throws the mirror across the room.

"Tess, it's badly swollen, and right now you can't see how it can be fixed—but it can. They will fix it." I take her hand and squeeze. "Okay, yes. You're going to look a fucking mess for a while, but you will get your old face back."

After saying this, I doubt her face will ever be the same. I'm trying to convince myself as well as Tessa that they can make her look like she did before.

"I don't have Riley to look beautiful for anymore, so why should I care?"

I'm glad Janet isn't here for this. She's sobbing and it's heartbreaking to see.

She looks at me, and at that moment we both feel

the enormity of our loss with the mention of Riley.

"Tess, all I've been sitting here thinking every day is that at least we have each other. I know in my heart that they will fix your face. We didn't lose each other. I'll be with you every step of the way."

She spends about ten minutes crying, cussing, and even slamming her left arm down on the bed in an effort to release some of the torment she must be feeling. She stares at me one last time, sucks in some air, and seems to shake it all off. With a small shake of her head, she tries to sit up a little straighter and says, "I could go for a cigarette. Actually, I could totally use a joint right about now."

We both start laughing.

"Oh God, don't make me laugh. It like feels like my mangled-ass face is ripping."

She starts to double over with laughter as I put my head down on her bed, trying to get control of myself too. Leave it to Tessa to bring us to hilarity in the worst situation ever. This is the spirit she needs to get through everything coming her way. My fighter of a best friend still has the grit that makes her Tessa.

Lonnie and Janet both walk in, holding what looks like soup from the cafeteria as Tessa and I are trying to contain ourselves. When they see us smiling, I can see the look of relief all over their faces.

Janet glances at the mirror laying on the floor across the room. "Honey, you know…"

Tessa interrupts her. "I know, Mom. They can fix it, or at least that's what Megan says. And you can't argue with Megan Shine because she knows everything."

"Exactly. Now eat your soup and shush it." I take one of the containers of soup from Janet and set it on the table next to Tessa's bed.

Tessa looks at the soup and back at me. "Soup?

Really? I was hoping for a burger right about now."

This makes us all laugh.

\*\*\*\*

Riley's funeral is the one of the saddest funerals I've ever been to. No kid should ever be in a coffin let alone a closed coffin because they were thrown through a windshield. Tessa's still in the hospital and isn't able to attend, which broke her heart further. Lindsey and I sat in the back, because I couldn't handle all the emotion. Jason should be here mourning his best friend with us. It's an odd feeling because in my mind I know he's gone, too.

Jason deserved a funeral like this. He deserved a flower-covered coffin and all of his friends gathered to say goodbye. Jason's mother couldn't afford one, nor did she have the money to even bury him. She had him cremated and that was it. My closure has been stolen from me. Saying goodbye at a funeral was what people needed. Funerals help you feel like the person you loved has moved on and you can someday start that process as well. Not having one for Jason makes me feel stuck.

After we leave the funeral, I ask Lindsey to drive me over to Jason's house. I want something of his for my own, something to give me some sort of closure. Lindsey agreed to drop me off at the top of the street. She hates Kenny so much that she won't even pull in his driveway.

\*\*\*\*

Kenny's in a drug-induced stupor with three other guys slumped on the couch in the living room when I get there. His mom needs to grow up and do some parenting for once. I can't even look at him, even though I know he's hurting. Like Lindsey, I'm done with the Evans family if Jason's no longer in it.

Not even asking permission, I go straight to Jason's room and try not to inhale. If I catch even a tiny trace of his vanilla votive candle mixed with the faint aroma of cigarette smoke, I'll lose it. Just being in his room is enough to send me over the edge. His bed looks like it did the last time I was here spending the day cuddling with strep throat. I shiver from the sorrow, trying to block the memory that's making my heart want to shut down.

There's a purple teddy bear on the table next to his couch, and the minute I see it my heart goes into overdrive. A tiny box with ribbon binds the arms of the bear together likes it's hugging itself. When I open the box there's a set of delicate, amethyst earrings sitting inside. My hands are shaking as I carefully take them out and put them on. This must've been my Christmas present. Until now, I forgot that he told me the next time I came over he had something for me. I can barely bring myself to walk out of his room because it's like I'm walking away from him forever even though he's already gone.

With my eyes blurred from the tears flowing out of them, I stride toward the living room and out of the house without even a glance at Kenny. He mumbles something to me as I walk out, but I keep on going.

Lindsey's still waiting for me at the top of the street. Opening her car door, I fall into the seat. I hold the bear up, unable to speak, and she immediately pulls my hair away from my face so she can see my ears.

"You knew about the earrings?" I ask her.

"Yeah, he's been helping Riley's dad rebuild a truck engine to afford them. He swore me to secrecy. They look beautiful on you."

I flip down her visor and look in the small mirror. "They're so perfect." I'm wiping my eyes so I can see them better. "I swear I'm never taking them off."

She smiles at me, starting her car. "I believe

you."

I want to go home and get in bed. I never knew that sorrow could exhaust you this much. I've been feeling like a zombie most of the time at school. I'm still feeling sick to my stomach off-and-on. I guess I have some sort of grief flu.

****

By the time Tessa's able to come home from the hospital, she still needs around-the-clock care. She needs help bathing and help getting around in general. Having a broken arm and collarbone makes it hard to do anything. She can't leave the house to do much aside from her hospital appointments. With her face still damaged, she doesn't want to leave the house right now anyway.

I'm beginning to worry because I've called over there every day for the last week and Janet tells me she's sleeping. How can she be asleep all the time? I get that she's on major pain medication, but this is ridiculous. Finally, after a whole week of not being able to talk to her, I call Janet and inform her I'm coming to visit Friday after school. Since second grade I've never gone this long without talking to Tessa, and I'm freaking out to say the least.

It nags at me that when I called Janet to let her know I was coming she acted weird about it. She almost seemed to hesitate when I told her. She said, "Uh, okay, sure. That would be good." And that's all she said. Tessa could be over there thinking I don't even care about her. Janet wouldn't want her to feel like that though. So, what is it? Something bad's happening, and I don't know what the hell it is, but by God I'm going to find out.

175

## Chapter Nineteen

Tessa's propped up in her bed with a dozen pillows watching TV when I walk into her room. Even after spending so many days with her at the hospital, I'm still taken off guard at the sight of her banged-up face. Her dad moved the living room TV up to her room so that she has something to do. They have a little table set up by her bed where she has some water, snacks, and a stack of magazines.

The whole ride over here I told myself to act normal. I'm not going to question why I haven't heard from her. For Tessa's sake, I need to hang with her and not try to immediately find out why Janet seems to be blocking us from talking. Maybe Tessa has no clue, but she has to wonder where I've been for over a week now.

Putting my hands on my hips, I survey her room. "Well they have you set up like the Queen of England in here, so it can't be all bad."

"Yeah right," she says, but with none of the Tessa sarcasm I know and love.

"You feeling okay? I've been thinking of you like every minute this week. I could barely concentrate at school." What's happening right now? She isn't happy to see me.

"At least you get to go to school." She doesn't look at me.

"Tess?" I force myself in her line of vision.

"Meg, I can't deal right now." She turns away from me and stares blankly out her window.

"Well, okay, I get that. You've been through hell, and I'm here with you. We'll get through all of this together." I'm relieved that she just seems super lost about everything, and that it has nothing to do with me.

She turns back to me and her eyes are filled with

anger and tears. "We? We aren't both in bed looking like a deformed monster. I'm stuck like this, Megan, not you!"

It's like she slapped me in the face. I'm shocked at her rage toward me. "I know that, Tess. I only meant I'm not gonna let you be alone while you have to go through all these surgeries. I know you're stuck in bed, and I'll sit here every night with you if I have to so you know you're not alone. Okay?" She isn't responding to me. "Tess?"

"Maybe you should, like, go right now." She starts crying.

"Go? I'm not leaving you. I'm not standing here pretending to know what it feels like to be you right now, but I'm here. You can't shut me out. Best friends don't leave. There is no way tha—"

"Please go." She interrupts me. "I can't handle all this right now."

"Handle what? What do you mean?" I'm getting mad now. "I didn't know our friendship turned into a burden for you." Standing at the foot of her bed, I'm helpless. I continue staring at her, unsure of what to do next.

"Please," she says once more, turning away from me again.

I walk to her bedroom door. I can't believe she actually wants me to leave.

"Okay I'll go, but I love you, and I'm coming back soon. Do you hear me?"

She doesn't say anything.

I walk out and rush to the front door. I can't face Janet right now. Dad dropped me off on his way to work a power outage, so I can't call him for a ride. I'm freezing my ass off trying to remember how close a gas station is. I find a payphone to call Lindsey's house—

177

thank God she's home. Standing there in the cold waiting for Lindsey to come pick me up, I've never experienced such confusion. Grandma's gone, Jason's gone, and now Tessa's choosing to shut me out.

****

I'm emotionally drained by the time I get back home.

Lindsey tried her best to soothe me with music and cheery conversation on the way to drop me off, but I'm a lunatic right now.

Chelsea's putting Zachary to bed, and she's surprised to see me.

I have no words for why I'm home and not staying at Tessa's like I told her I was. My life is like a house that someone picked up and shook everything out of and then set it back down empty. I'm completely stripped of everything that matters.

Going in the bathroom to wash my face and get ready for bed feels like a chore at this point.

Chelsea comes in and starts dousing a cotton ball with her Sea Breeze.

It reeks like the cleaning supplies grandma always used, and the aroma makes me feel like I'm going to throw up. "I'm not sure what's going on with you, but since you're home, I think I'm going to go to Erica's. I need a break from this house."

I shrug and start brushing my hair back into a pony.

"Meg? You okay?" She has gone from bossy to *uh oh something's not right*.

All I can manage to do is shake my head no. Words won't come out. The more I hold it in the more I start to shake all over. This must be what a nervous breakdown feels like.

She grabs me by the shoulders and ushers me into

my room.

Once she sits me down on my bed, she says, "Is it Jason? Are you having a moment about Jason?"

"It's not Jason," I finally say through tears. "I mean yes it's always Jason, but Tessa won't..." I can't get it out. How do I explain what happened with me and Tessa?

"Tessa won't what?" She sits down beside me.

"She told me to leave." When I say this, I roll back on my bed and cry into my pillow.

"Leave? You mean she told you to leave when you got to her house tonight?"

I lift the pillow off my face and nod before I cover it back up.

"Well, maybe she's out of sorts from all the pain pills she's living on."

I sit up. "No, you don't understand. She was mean to me, like she wasn't Tessa." Trying to calm down so she can understand me, I explain what happened.

She's staring at me cool and calm, trying to think of something to say to make me feel better. The nausea that has been hitting me for two weeks moves through me again. It's been awful today. All this grief is making me physically sick.

"Do you think maybe she's only moody from all she's going through? She could also be getting ready to get her period. You know when you get your period, you're impossible to talk to for like a week before."

Is she kidding me? Chelsea is a raging bitch right before her period. All of a sudden alarm bells go off in my head. When was my last period? I don't remember having my period at all since right after Thanksgiving. My last period ended right before I got strep throat. I remember because I asked Bertie to pick up some pads for Chelsea when she went to get my antibiotics, since I used them all the week before.

I stand and go get my purse off the dresser to find my birth-control pack, tucked inside a hidden pocket. Pulling out the pill pack, I start counting the days. Yep. I'd missed my period and must've started a new pack without even thinking about it in all the chaos of the last month.

"What's wrong? You look like you might be sick. Meg, you're scaring me." She's furrowing her brow.

"I missed my period. Have you ever missed a period since you started the pill?"

"No. Mine comes every twenty-one days on my pill," she says, trying to peer at my pill pack.

"Me too. Mine is the same, remember?" I hold up my pill pack to show her.

"Well, maybe it's stress. I mean, you're on the pill, so it shouldn't be anything to worry about."

She's trying to assure me, but I'm still worried. I nod. "Yeah. You're right. Maybe my body freaked out with this weird flu crap, and I must have missed it."

Putting my pill pack back in my purse, I notice she looks stressed now.

"When you say you've had the flu, what do you mean?"

"You know, I've felt pukey and light-headed for a while," I say, looking at her, trying to understand her look of concern.

She's thinking about what I said. "You don't mean you feel like someone who might have morning sickness, do you?"

Looking at her, I think about that for a second. "No. It isn't only the morning. It's off-and-on all day. I have it right now actually."

"Meg, don't you remember grandma once told us that morning sickness can be all-day sickness? She said she was sick day-and-night when she was pregnant with dad and Aunt Karen, and she knew they were going to be a handful. Morning sickness happening only in the morning is an old-wives tale according to grandma."

"What are you saying? You think I could be pregnant?" I start to sweat and stand up. I go over and open my bedroom window.

"Let's think about this for a minute," she says, motioning for me to come sit on the bed by her. "When was your last period?"

"Right before I had strep throat—like six weeks ago."

"Okay. And you've taken your pill every day at the same time and haven't missed any at all?"

"Yes. You know I'm obsessive about that." I stand back up and pace again.

"We're not going to panic, but I think you should take a pregnancy test to be safe."

"*What?* Are you crazy?" I yell, not meaning to.

"*Shh.* You're going to wake Zach."

"Chelsea! I don't need a test! I'm on the pill!"

"First of all, you need to stop yelling. Second, please come sit down and stop pacing because you're making me nervous."

Sitting down beside her, I instantly start crying. "Please tell me something that'll make this be okay. I can't be pregnant. I'm on the pill, and I haven't been with Jason since before Christmas. I mean, there is like zero chance you can get pregnant on the pill unless you don't take it correctly, and I take it correctly. Right?"

Chelsea's silently thinking this over.

I lay back on my bed and my mind is racing. My thoughts jump from Dad killing me and then to Jason. I need Jason here with me. I need to call him and tell him what's happening right now. He would rush over and help me calm down, I know he would. Why the hell did I turn him away when he came to my window that night? I would do anything to do that night over. That was the last time I saw him, and I turned him away.

"I'm going to call the pharmacy and ask them if it's at all possible to get pregnant on the pill." She's trying to sound confidant about this decision.

"Are you serious?"

"What the hell else can we do? We can't call Mom!" She is starting to freak out too.

"I can't believe we're going to do this."

She gets up and walks out of my room.

"Hey, where are you going?"

"I have to go find the phone book unless you know the number to the pharmacy by heart."

*Obviously, I have no clue what the number is, ass face.* "Okay."

Chelsea comes back in lugging the humongous phone book with her. She pages through it, reciting the alphabet in her head so she can find the number.

*Good God why is it taking you so long to find a phone number.*

"Can you call them for me?" I ask, knowing this is going to irritate the hell out of her. I need Tessa right now, dammit!

She points to a number in the phone book, picks up the phone, and dials. "Yes, hi. I was wondering if I could talk to the doctor ... I mean pharmacist about a medication." She looks at me. "You owe me big time for this."

"I know," I say.

When the pharmacist comes on, Chelsea asks what could cause a missed period when you take birth control pills. She tells him the exact name of the pill. I assume it's a he, but maybe not.

"Yes, uh huh." She nods. "Wow, okay, I didn't know that. Uh huh, yes."

I'm getting impatient. What the heck is he saying to her?

"I will ask her these questions and do as you suggest. Thank you." She hangs up.

"Well? What did he say?" I'm wringing my hands together.

"He told me to ask you the following questions." She clears her throat and sits up straight like she's in a job interview. "First, have you had any spotting because you might have had a light period due to stress?"

"No spotting that I remember at all."

"Second, did you miss any pills, but I know you didn't so we can skip that one. Third, do you recall a time in the last couple of months when you took the pill and then maybe had a bit of diarrhea or any vomiting? Who on God's green Earth knew that taking the pill and then getting sick an hour or so after can make the pill not as effective, by the way?"

"No. I started feeling sick to my stomach, but that was about a month after my last period."

"Okay and fourth..." She freezes, and looks at me with the biggest, wide-eyed expression I've ever seen. "Oh shit."

"Oh shit what? What? What is oh shit!" I'm about to smack her to get her to speak.

"He said a round of antibiotics can reduce the pill's protection. Strep throat—you took them for strep throat. Oh my god."

"What? Seriously? Oh no, oh no, oh no."

Erica comes walking in my room. "What the hell is going on? You both look like you just saw the devil sitting in the living room."

"We need to go to the pharmacy and buy a

pregnancy test," Chelsea says to Erica with her eyes glued to mine.

## Chapter Twenty

Waiting for Chelsea and Erica to get back feels like when your best pair of jeans are in the dryer too damp to wear and you're late for school—one minute feels like an hour. Trying to talk myself down, I wander in circles around my house, crying and basically flipping out. I think about calling Tessa, but if she still doesn't want to talk to me that would make this worse. I need to talk to her though.

Piss on it, I'm calling her.

"Hello?"

"Hi, Janet, can I talk to Tess?"

"Megan you sound like you're crying. Is everything all right honey?"

*Besides the fact that Tessa basically kicked me out earlier, and oh I might be pregnant and also my boyfriend died?*

"No. Yes. I'm fine. Can I talk to Tess?"

"I'm sorry, honey, she's asleep."

*You're lying to me, dammit.*

"Will you tell her I need to talk to her when she wakes up?"

She hesitates. "Yes, I'll tell her. Take care, hon." She hangs up.

*Argh!* I do feel worse now!

By the time Chelsea gets back with Erica, I've worked myself into a complete frenzy.

"What in the name of everything holy took you so long?" I'm breathing heavy and sweating.

Chelsea looks me up and down. "You're going to need to calm down so we can do this. Erica has actually taken one of these before, so she's going to help you." Chelsea hands the sack to Erica.

I look at Erica.

"Hey, no judging, I had a scare last year." Erica reaches in the bag and pulls out two pregnancy test boxes like she's pulling out two big macs from a McDonalds sack—no big deal.

"We bought two tests because you're supposed to take the test first thing in the morning. Something about the first mornings pee or some weird shit like that. I figure we'd take one tonight, and when that one is negative, we'll take another first thing in the morning to make doubly sure."

She hands me the first box, and I'm staring at the box in my hand, wondering how I got here. I pull out the plastic stick thingy. "You pee on this thing?" I ask, holding up the test.

"Yep. Go in, do your business, and then bring it back out here—we can wait together." Erica goes to sit on my bed with Chelsea.

Chelsea looks like she's going to have a meltdown. "Hello? What are you waiting for? Hurry your ass up," she says to me.

She's just as freaked out as me because she knows dad will kill me.

In the bathroom, sitting down on the toilet, my hands are trembling as I place the stick in my stream of pee. I'm getting pee all over my hand as I soak the test. I go until I don't have any left. With my hands still shaking, I put the cap back on the test and set it on the bathroom floor gently so it doesn't screw up the results if that even matters.

Taking a pregnancy test isn't very clean when you have to put a lid on a pee-soaked stick. While I wash my hands, I catch a glimpse of my reflection in the mirror. Leftover makeup's smeared down my face, and I look like the lead singer of KISS. I make out the bright, pink plus-sign in the test window before I bend over to pick it up.

I'm stunned into silence and I walk like a robot out of bathroom. Willing it to change, I keep staring at the little test window. I even start wondering if I'm crazy, and I'm imagining the extra line forming the cross on the positive sign. I blow on the test window hoping that will do something to change the result.

"Meg?" Chelsea stands up and comes over to me. "Why the hell are you blowing on it? Is it starting to show anything yet?"

Erica snatches the test out of my hand. "*Holy* shit!" She grabs the box the test came in, reads it again, and looks back at the stick.

"You're totally prego."

"What the hell are you talking about? She can't be pregnant!" Chelsea yanks the test from Erica's hand.

It's like she all of a sudden forgot that the pharmacy said my birth control could be cancelled out from the antibiotics I took. The pharmacy said it's a bad combination. They should call it a life changing combination—bad combination doesn't do this situation justice.

"This can't be possible," Chelsea says again.

"I mean obviously it's possible," Erica says to nobody in particular.

We ignore her.

"What am I going to do?" I feel like a caged animal, like I can't get enough air. I begin hyperventilating.

"What do you mean what are you going to do?" Chelsea takes the test and the box and stuffs it all in my top sock drawer, fearing dad could walk in any minute.

"I'm pregnant!" How am I going to do this?" I look from Erica to Chelsea.

Erica puts both her arms up like *don't look at me.*

"Do what?" Chelsea finally asks me.

"Have a baby!" I'm yelling at them both now.

"Have you momentarily lost your mind? You aren't having a baby. There's no way on God's green earth you can raise a child at sixteen, nor will Dad even allow you to do that. You have to get an abortion. Oh, Jesus where will we get the money for an abortion." Chelsea stands and begins to pace too.

"Abortion?" I say.

"Yes, an abortion. Jessica McMurray had one in tenth grade. You don't need a parent, but she told us girls that you have to have the cash," Chelsea says.

"They're not cheap either," Erica adds.

"What about Jason?" As I say his name it hits me that his baby is currently swimming around in my body. I start hyperventilating again with huge whooshes of air strangling me. I'm chocking on my own air.

Leave it to Chelsea to not even consider that this is Jason's baby or consider how I feel. I get that she's operating from reality but still.

"Do you think you can live at home, and go to school, and Dad's going to help you? Do you think that you'll go off to school every day while the nanny keeps your kid and Zachary? What are you thinking? Tell me right now, because obviously you're not thinking straight at all."

I try to slow my breathing so I can speak. "I'm thinking that I have Jason's baby inside me right now. I can't think about anything else."

Chelsea softens her tone when she realizes it's also about Jason. "Meg. I get that this is excruciating, but you have to think of your future. And God, how will you ever survive trying to raise a kid without any help?"

"I don't know! I don't know!" I'm so hysterical that Erica stands and then sits back down real fast, unsure of what to do with herself.

"I think if Jason were here, he wouldn't want you to give up your dreams of college because you guys made a mistake." She's trying hard to convince me without yelling at me.

"To be honest, I know if Jason were here, he would never see this as a mistake. We tried to protect ourselves from this, and it still happened." I take another huge breath in and blow it out. "Maybe I can have the baby. If I put the baby up for adoption I can still go to college." I don't even know what I'm saying or what it means for me.

Chelsea's silent before she says, "If you go through with the pregnancy and put the baby up for adoption, you will have to tell dad. Everyone will know! Dad will never allow this."

"It's not Dad's choice. It's my choice. He can't force me to do anything." I use the blanket on my bed to wipe my runny nose.

"What if you hide it from him?" Erica speaks up.

"What?" Chelsea and I speak at the same time. I think we forgot she was still here for a minute.

"Well, what if you hide the pregnancy from your dad until you get a plan together."

"What do you mean a plan?" Chelsea plops down on my floor, looking at Erica.

"It will give you time to explore adoption without the pressure of your dad."

Who knew Erica could be so sensible?

"Yeah, exactly. I need time to see what adoption options I have," I say to Chelsea.

"That would require adult help. We have no adult!" Chelsea's getting worked up again.

"*So*, we're sure we can't ask your mom?" We both look at Erica. "Right, okay I was just asking. How about all the different pamphlets at the clinic about adoption. I could drive us there Monday after school to get some."

I nod my head. "Oh my God, yes. I need to see what all the options are." I look at Chelsea. "Can you please give me some time to figure out what to do before you jump back on the abortion train?"

"I'm not on the abortion train, but you can't have a baby." Chelsea looks at Erica for help.

"That's the same thing as an abortion," I say.

"Look you have known you're pregnant for like ten minutes. Your dad can't tell you're pregnant. None of us can tell you're pregnant, including you, so you both need to calm down and think about it all. You don't have to decide tonight. I mean I think you're screwed either way, but you still have some time," Erica says, looking from Chelsea to me and back to Chelsea.

"Wow, thanks for that last part," I say to Erica, knowing she's right.

"Fine. We'll go get the stupid pamphlets Monday and go from there." Chelsea frowns at me with so much pity that it actually makes me feel better. It means she cares.

"I did what I was supposed to do. I took the fucking pill, and I still got pregnant. What else could I have done?"

"I know you did, but we can't worry about that now. We have to figure out what to do now. We'll give you some space, but come down to my room if you want to talk it through some more," Chelsea says.

I'm crying into my hands when Chelsea and Erica walk out of my room, closing the door behind them.

Debating on trying to call Tessa again, I figure she probably really is asleep now. I don't want to wake Lindsey either because I was such a nutcase when she picked me up from Tessa's, and I don't want to bother her again.

Thinking about Jason, I remember one night on one of our late-night phone calls, Jason and I actually talked about kids. To my surprise, he told me he wanted three kids someday. He said he always felt like he needed one more sibling. I thought he wanted one more sibling to help him deal with Kenny and his mom, but he just said three was the perfect number in his mind. Agreeing with him, I said three kids was the right amount in my mind too. For me, it was what I was used to, I suppose. He told me this meant we were destined to be together. I hung up the phone that night wondering if we would stay together through school and end up married with kids.

Lifting my shirt up to my chest, I stand to get a better view of my bare belly. I don't notice a difference. Rubbing my hand against it, I jiggle it really fast, but I don't feel any movement inside. Did the baby feel that? Maybe I just deformed the baby by shaking my stomach like a crazy person. Great, I'm already a complete failure as a mom. It hits me in that moment that I'm going to be a mom. I want to have this baby.

I drop my shirt back down and look at my face in my bedroom mirror. Turning my face side to side, I don't see it. I don't look like I could be a mom, just a teenage girl who has English homework due Monday. Erica's right, dad won't be able to tell I'm pregnant. I can't tell, and I'm the one who's actually pregnant. I've never needed or wanted anyone like I want Jason right now.

The fear taking over me is like no other fear I've felt before. Sure, I've been afraid of things before, but knowing another human is going to depend on me is off the charts terrifying. I'm going to be on my own, and it's like jumping off a cliff with nothing to catch you and no end in sight.

The loud rumble of my dad's Bronco startles me as I hear him pull up. It brings the fear to a whole new level. Feeling myself start to tremble at the thought of having to tell him someday soon, I shut my eyes tight. He drops his keys on the kitchen table, and comes down the hall. I know he won't come in my room with my light off, but I pull the covers over my head anyway, wishing I could disappear.

## Chapter Twenty-One

As I walk cautiously into the living room the next morning, I have that feeling you get when you're home alone and completely freaked out that there's a stranger just waiting around the corner to attack you. My dad is working through his normal Saturday morning routine—wad of paper towels in one hand—Windex bottle in the other. He jazzes, somewhat on beat, around to the Doobie Brother's song playing as he sprays the entire living room down. Leaving him to his cleaning ritual of covering every surface with glass cleaner, I head back to the safety of my room. I know he doesn't know I'm pregnant, but I still feel scared.

"What the hell?" My dad projects from behind me, and I freeze.

"Hell, hell, hell." Zachary repeats him with enthusiasm.

"No, no, no, we don't say hell."

Realizing he's not yelling at me, I scurry down the hall.

I sit on my bed, and I don't know what to do with myself. I'm not sure why because in my dad's mind nothing has changed, but I still feel like I'm in trouble. I remember when my parents were still married, and I did something to piss my mom off. She'd tell me to go to my room until my dad came home to deal with me.

I'd watch out the window the whole evening, fretting and shaking, because I knew a spanking was coming my way when he got home from work. Sure enough, he would come in, turn me around, and give me three hard swats. Telling me I better knock it off, he would go back down the hall, leaving my door open after he went. I was always afraid that I'd get another spanking for leaving the room, even though he never said

I had to stay in there.

Having that same feeling of dread now like I should stay in my room, I'm counting down the hours until he goes to bed—it's going to be a long day. As I throw myself onto my bed in an attempt to go back to sleep, there's a scratch at my door. I lift my head and look toward it. The scratching is louder this time.

"Gan, it me. Gannnnnnnn!" Zachary goes from scratching to banging the door within seconds.

He comes scurrying over to me, and I catch him in my arms, curling his warm body into my lap. He nuzzles into me, wrapping his arms around my throat. The look on his face is one of mischief. I'm not sure what he's up to, but I'm sure it's not good. He smells like maple syrup, which could either mean his diaper is full of pee or he had pancakes for breakfast. Why I think the two scents are alike on a toddler beats me, but they are.

"Meg? Hello?" My dad is hollering down the hall for me.

"Uh, yeah?" I peek my head out of my room.

"Is your brother in there with you?"

"Uh, yeah." I don't know why I can't manage to say anything else at the moment.

"Okay, for a second I thought he was downstairs with the Windex. He got away from me apparently." Zachary's like a lightning bug trapped in a jar, constantly moving and bouncing off every surface.

"He's with me, and no Windex in sight." I quickly take a look down the hall to see if he ditched the Windex on the way to my room.

I hear my dad say to himself, "Then where the hell is the damn Windex?" Then he addresses me. "Anyway, do you have plans to be at Tessa's today?"

It's like a stab to my heart, because normally I would have plans with Tessa. I'm shocked that he's acting like it's not a big deal for me to have plans with Tessa. The accident has changed his attitude when it comes to me being with her. He flipped out when he found out Janet was letting her date, but now I guess with the shape Tessa's in, and Riley not being here, it's not an issue anymore.

"Actually, no. She's not doing the best and needs to rest according to Janet." I can't tell him what's really going on. I don't really know what's really going on.

"If you're staying here can you watch Zachary? I have some errands to run, and I'd rather not drag him with me. It's too cold, and it'll take me double the time bringing him along." He asks this question like I have a choice.

*Sure. I have no life anyway and thanks for your concern about Tessa.*

"Okay, yeah," I say.

"Maybe we can get a game of Scrabble in tonight, eh?" He turns the living room stereo back up as the vacuum cleaner roars to life.

Chelsea's probably livid that he's being so loud this early in the morning.

*Scrabble? Are you kidding me?* It's like he thinks I'm fine. My boyfriend died and my best friend went through a traumatic accident, and he wants to play games. The last thing I want to do is play anything with him. Keeping up with the charade that everything is okay is all I can do. I don't want him even the least bit curious of something going on with me—for now anyway.

****

Chelsea comes upstairs wearing only a Culture Club t-shirt and underwear. Her hair's a nest of blonde curls piled around her head, and she looks like she's been up all night like I have. I'm trying to keep Zachary occupied by letting him spray the Windex that he,

195

apparently, did snatch from dad and hid in the kitchen cabinet. The kid's smarter than we think. He can't really get any Windex to come out of the sprayer, but he thinks he can so I'm good with it.

Chelsea goes to the fridge and peeks inside. When she sees there's only butter and milk in there, she closes it with a sigh. "What the hell are we supposed to eat, and why the hell was dad blaring his damn stereo while I was trying to sleep?"

"Well good morning to you too."

She opens up the pantry to find a big box of nothing.

I like that she thinks dad should wait until she decides to wake up to get his chores done. She's such a princess. "Dad's at the store right now, so it's either a bowl full of milk or suck on a stick of butter until he gets back," I say. The thought of butter makes me want to gag. I'm already feeling nauseous this morning and eating isn't on my radar. When does this sickness get better? At this rate I'm not gaining pregnancy weight, I'm losing it.

She looks at me, and then she goes back down to her room.

Geez, I guess I've already managed to piss her off. Shouldn't she be a little more sympathetic? I did have a nervous breakdown last night after all. Actually, I could have another one at any given moment. My emotions are a rollercoaster of instability just waiting to come rolling out.

"Since dad's not home, I wanna go over some of this information." She's back upstairs with pamphlets in her hand, and she's wearing sweatpants thank God.

"Where did you get these?" I ask.

"I forgot that when I went to get on the pill last year, I saved all these clinic handouts." She spreads them out on the table in front of me in a professional manner, acting like she's my interior decorator and we're picking out wallpaper.

"Chelsea, these are all about abortion."

There's one that's about what to do before your appointment and another one for abortion after care. One of the pamphlets has a picture of a teen girl with her mom's arm around her shoulders sitting at a doctor's office. Nobody has a parent take them to get an abortion. In Missouri it's like a secret—we know better than to involve parents. The picture should be a group of teen girls all sitting together looking scared shitless.

"Did you think you were pregnant before? Were these for you?" I'm confused as to why she was holding onto abortion pamphlets from a year ago.

"No, but when Erica had her scare last year it made me think about what I would do if I ever did get pregnant," she says. "It's good to be prepared, I guess."

"Oh." I pretend to sift through all the information. I'm waiting for the right moment to tell her I've decided to keep Jason's baby. If she would stop babbling on about abortion, I could tell her now.

"Anyway, Erica said that she remembers calling and asking how much it would cost." She lets out a heavy breath. "It's going to be about two hundred dollars. Since you're not that far along it will be cheaper than most."

"*What?* That's insane."

"What if we ask Bertie to borrow the money? We can trust that she won't tell dad, and you can get a job this year to pay her back," she says.

"I'm not asking Bertie for money." I pull my knees up to my chest and stare at the floor.

"We have no choice if we're going to hide this from dad. He arranged for Bertie to bring over beef stroganoff and a cake for you tonight. It's for your birthday."

I haven't given my birthday any thought. It just seems like another day without Tessa around to celebrate it. With it being on Valentine's Day that just depresses me further not having Jason here.

"Seriously? That's what we're doing for my 16th birthday? Having dinner with dad and Bertie? I'd rather do nothing to be honest."

"Sorry. It was supposed to be a surprise. I know its lame, but it's not like he was going to let you have a party, not that you even wanted one. When she comes over, we can find a way to ask her."

"This sucks."

"Hey, at least you're not Samantha Baker. They didn't fucking forget your birthday," she says, quoting Molly Ringwald in Sixteen Candles. She thinks this is funny and then when I don't crack a smile, she says, "Sorry."

"Chelsea, I'm not having an abortion. I'm just not." I stare straight into her eyes so she knows this isn't up for debate.

"Meg, stop living in a fantasy land and come back to Earth. You're getting ready to be sixteen. You can't have a baby."

"I'm not changing my mind. I'm having this baby. This baby is all that I have left of Jason." I'm proud of myself because for the first time in months I manage not to cry when I think of Jason.

Chelsea pauses and then stands up. "I can't even talk to you right now. You clearly need more time to get it together." She scoops up the pamphlets and turns to go. I don't see anger on her face, what I see is worry.

Looking around the living room, she asks, "Is Zach with Dad?"

"Oh shit." I tear down the hall to find Zachary. God only knows what he has gotten into now. Rounding the corner into my room, the strong aroma of nail polish hits me before I get to him.

"Paintin Gan. Pwetty." Zachary stands up, and he's covered in nail polish. There are multiple bottles with the lids screwed off laying on my bedspread. He looks like a rainbow landed on his head and melted all over him—his face is five different colors.

Chelsea walks in behind me. "Wow, like wow," she says. "You can't keep track of Zachary for an hour, but you want to have a baby."

"Fuck off." I shoot her the dirtiest look I've ever given anyone in my life.

"Buck off," Zachary repeats, continuing to paint his face.

"You're going to be mother of the year." She walks out of my room as I throw one of the bottles of nail polish—that still has the lid on thankfully—at her.

Feeling tears starting, I wipe them away so Zachary doesn't get upset. I have to get stronger than I am, if not for me, for my brother. I lead him out of my room, holding onto his hand so he doesn't run off and get nail polish everywhere, and head for the bathroom. How will I ever get this kid back to one color again? He looks ridiculous. I'm pretty sure he even painted his eyelids.

As I look down at him, he smiles up at me. "I'm pwetty, Gan."

"You are something, that's for sure." I smile back at him. This is just another ordinary day in the Shine house. I don't see why we don't have room for one more.

## Chapter Twenty-Two

Monday morning, I wake up before school feeling like I've been on a boat out at sea for days. I'm dizzy and off balance. The whole ride to school, I think I might hurl all over the bus. Erica usually gives me and Chelsea a ride to school, but I'm running late thanks to feeling so awful. To top it off, I had a dream about Jason last night, and I can't shake the aftermath of sadness still lingering.

The dream wasn't about the baby or anything about the accident. In the dream, Jason shows up to my school. He's standing at my locker, and I'm surprised to see him. He tells me he's going to come to school with me now because he didn't want me to be alone anymore. It's like he had been on a trip or something because in the dream I keep asking him when he got back.

I woke up heartbroken and pissed that it wasn't real. I tried falling back to sleep, hoping to be thrown right back into my dream so I could spend more time with Jason.

****

I go to the gym to call Tessa during lunch—there's no way I can handle the smell of the cafeteria right now. There's a line at the payphones that I don't have time to wait in, but I'm desperate to talk to her. The girl hogging the phone in front of me is clearly talking to a guy, because she's flirting and acting like a moron. Did I act that way around Jason? No. I know I didn't, because this girl is highly annoying.

I tap her on the shoulder. "Hi, I'm sure your conversation is super important right now, but I have an actual emergency, and I need to use this phone." She doesn't appreciate the attitude I have going on, but I don't care.

She shoots me a dirty look over her shoulder, but wraps up her phone call, telling whoever she's talking to that a freak behind her needs the phone. I'm not going to waste my breath telling her to piss off. She gives me another dirty look and huffs off, which I respond to with my middle finger.

The phone rings for a while and right when I'm going to hang up, Tessa answers. "Hello?"

"Tess, thank God you answered."

"Meg?" She sounds kind of out of it, and I realize I must've woken her.

"Oh, Tess, I'm so sorry if I woke you up."

"Aren't you supposed to be at school?"

Just as she asks me that the gym teacher comes walking past me toward her office with a lunch tray in one hand and a Tab in the other. She glances at me, but I can tell she wants to eat her lunch in peace and not deal with anything else.

I give her a small wave as if to say I'll go back to wherever the hell I'm supposed to be in a minute so go eat your lunch. "I am at school. Look, I know you're going through something, well not something, but a lot of somethings. I really really need to talk to you, though." She sounds like she's breathing weird on the other end of the line. "Tess, you okay?"

There's more weird breathing. "No. I'm actually not okay. I have, like, a pretty major surgery on my face this weekend. Can I call you later or something?"

"Call me later? No, Tess, I'm not waiting until later to talk to you. I'm worried about you. What time is the surgery?" My need to talk with her has shifted from my emergency to whatever the hell is going on with her at the moment. I didn't know they moved her face surgery up, and I have to be there for her like I promised, even though she's making it impossible.

"How the hell do I know what time it is? It's Saturday, okay? I'm going to hang up now."

"No, wait. I swear to God if you hang up on me, I'm going to…" Then the dial tone assaults my ear. She must've hung up right after she finished talking. I don't think I have it in me to go back to class while my life falls apart with every passing minute. But I know nothing good will come of me skipping class.

Trudging to Algebra, I pass Chelsea in the hall. She's with a group of girls who are all talking at the same time. How do any of them keep up with the conversation? I give her a tiny wave, and she waves back, but worry creases her brow. Sadness must be written all over my face, because as I go into my class, she's still looking at me, walking backward down the hall.

I manage to get through the day, but one of my teachers asks me to stay after because he's concerned about me. I know that I've been acting abnormal, but I can't help it. I tell him I've been sick. I can't say, "Yeah, I'm going to have a baby and my dad's going to find out soon. So, I'm sorry for seeming out of it in class." I went with the lie which is easier on both of us. I'm not sure how I will get through this week of school with all I have going on inside me, and I'm still worried sick about Tessa.

\*\*\*\*

By the time dad drops me off at the hospital Saturday, Tessa's out of surgery. Janet called me during the week to let me know when the surgery was. I thought about asking Lindsey if she wanted to come, but I want to be alone with Tessa if she allows it.

I'm in the waiting room anxiously anticipating the results of how the surgery went when Janet walks by. "Janet!"

"Oh, Megan, honey, I didn't know you were already here."

I nod. "How is she?"

"Well, if you want to walk down to the cafeteria with me I can fill you in. Lonnie needs some caffeine, and I could go for an herbal tea."

*Lord, don't let the cafeteria smells make me puke*, I think but keep walking. "What all did they do to Tessa's face today?"

"They inserted a metal plate behind her eyebrow to help with the bone that was shattered there."

I stop walking for a second and look at Janet. I cringe at the thought of what Tessa went through but motion for Janet to keep talking.

"They say the metal plate will take away the sunken look she has on that eye. In a couple of weeks, they're going to take fat from her thigh and fill in the groove she has going down the side of her face. Once she heals from all that, she will begin to look more like her old self. It won't be perfect, but it will be much better."

I find a table once we get to the cafeteria while Janet orders.

She turns from the cashier and says, "Megan, honey, would you like anything?"

"No thank you." I can't stomach food right now.

She's the sweetest mother I've ever known. I think maybe after all this Tessa will appreciate her more than ever.

Sipping her tea, she comes to sit down at the table.

"Janet, I need you to tell me the truth about something." I'm struggling to make eye contact.

She doesn't act the least bit surprised. She must know what's coming.

"Tessa's shutting me out of her life and I don't

know why." Keeping with my usual ridiculousness of crying all the time, I wipe the tears from my eyes.

Janet digs a Kleenex out of her purse. I swear this woman has nothing but maternal bones in her body.

Reaching for the Kleenex, I try to pull myself together.

"There's something about the night of the accident you don't know."

I inhale sharply. What now? I can't handle much more. "Okay?" I say.

"That night, Riley and Jason both told Tessa there was no way they could leave and go to Erica's. They had heard from other kids that tried to leave and had come back to the party that the roads were a sheet of ice. Riley said he was not going to attempt that drive."

The mere mention of Jason's name makes my pulse speed up. He's gone, but he can still cause my heart to flutter. I don't say anything to Janet and wait for her to continue.

"She told Jason that he couldn't let you down and Jason talked Riley into leaving Paul's house."

"How do you know all this?" I'm picturing the conversation that went on the night of New Year's Eve. I know Tessa. If she puts her mind to something, she's relentless until she gets her way. Knowing how desperate I was to see Jason, she was trying to make me happy that night.

"When she stopped wanting to take your calls that's when I became aware her depression had reached a new level. She loves you as a sister, which is why she's shutting down from you."

"What do you mean?" I'm trying to understand what she's getting at.

Janet pats me on the hand and looks at me with the corners of her mouth curved upside down. "Tessa thinks it's all her fault. She blames herself for Riley's death, and the fact that you no longer have Jason."

I'm completely at a loss for words. I would never blame Tessa for this. That thought would never cross my mind. "None of this is her fault. It was an accident," I say.

"Honey, I have told her that a million times, but she believes it is. She thinks she has ruined your life, and she has so much guilt over Riley, too."

"That's not true. How was she supposed to know it would end this way? Riley never would've gone if he thought this would happen. How do I get through to her? I miss her, and I can't lose her. I've lost almost everyone I care about, and I can't stand the thought of Tessa blaming herself."

"I understand that, and you understand that, but Tessa does not. I think you need to keep calling her, and maybe in time she'll come around."

"Do you think she's awake right now?" I ask, remembering she's laying upstairs in a hospital bed.

"No. They're going to keep her sedated until tomorrow to help with the pain."

"Maybe I can leave her a note and tell her I love her. I want her to know I was here."

"That's a wonderful idea. Just seeing your handwriting will hopefully cheer her up. Our old Tessa is in there somewhere. We just have to bring her back out."

"I'm glad she doesn't hate me, because for a while there I was confused."

"She could never hate you." Janet gives my hand one last squeeze, and we head back down the hall to Tessa's room.

She's laying there with a bandage covering half of her face and head, and my heart aches to talk to her. She looks very peaceful, and I'm glad she's sedated.

Lonnie and Janet talk quietly to each other while I write her a note.

*Dear Tess,*

*I came by to argue with you about who wins worst week ever. My week has been pretty shitty. More on that later. I'm guessing since I'm here sitting next to you, and you don't even know it, I'll let you win this one. Also, the next time I come to see you, which will be soon, I'm totally painting your nails. Have you seen those things lately? What a mess! Haha. So, I need you to know that I love you, and I'll be thinking about you even when I'm not here. As you know, there's no getting rid of Megan Shine. Plus, I know you've seen the previews for the new Molly Ringwald movie Pretty in Pink, and I will kick your ass if you watch it without me. Okay that's all for now. Call me, day or night.*

*Love the Cameron to your Ferris,*

*Meg*

I hand the note to Janet and take one last glance at Tessa. I leave her room knowing I can't do anything more to fix this right now. I can only hope and pray like grandma would tell me to do. She would be proud to know her advice has stayed with me through all of this. That's what grandmas are best at—leaving you with the tools to cope with life when it doesn't make sense. Nothing in my life makes sense right now.

## Chapter Twenty-Three

It's weird being back at the clinic again. The last time I was here it was to get birth control. That obviously didn't go as planned. Erica gave Chelsea and I a ride because I decided—and made Chelsea come with me—that I needed to see the doctor and confirm what we already pretty much know—I'm pregnant. I just thought it should be official, and that meant I had to see a doctor.

After the nurse gives me a test to confirm my pregnancy, the doctor comes in. He looks at both of us sitting in the room and lets out a big irritated sigh, like here we go again more pregnant teens who didn't take their birth control.

Chelsea folds her arms and huffs right back at him.

In a manner that seems more like a lecture than anything else, he asks me a bunch of questions about when I had my last period. When I tell him about the birth control mishap, he starts digging through my file to find the date that I took the antibiotics. He's acting shocked that I'm pregnant, and he's kind of being a jerk to me. I want to say, "Listen, asshole, if you would've told me that an antibiotic could cancel out birth control, maybe this wouldn't have happened."

Instead, I sit on the exam table giving him dirty looks right along with Chelsea. He's being rude to the wrong girls—we don't take any crap. We're not going to be treated like irresponsible idiots when we thought we were being responsible in the first place.

He roots around in the drawer behind him, and pulls out some sort of contraption. He directs me to lie back and lift my shirt up. "I want to see if we can get a listen to the heartbeat," he says.

I look over at Chelsea. I don't think either one of

us expected this today.

He rubs some sort of probe over my belly and then a whirring sound fills the room.

"Is that the heartbeat?" I ask.

He nods and I'm in awe. I can actually hear the baby's—my baby's—heart beating. He quickly takes the probe off my belly and says, "The baby's heart is beating at one hundred and forty-two beats a minute."

I wasn't done listening, and he doesn't give two shits about that. I ask, "Is that good?"

"Yes, it is." He is being very matter of fact.

I want to say, "Sorry we interrupted your day and made you do your job."

Chelsea's silent as he gets a medical pad out and quickly jots something down.

"Okay, Megan, this is your due date from what I gather by your period dates and the heartbeat." He flippantly hands me the piece of paper. He tells me to take it with me when I make an appointment with the pregnancy doctor. As if I have a pregnancy doctor.

When I look down and see the date written on the paper, I almost fall off the exam table. The writing on the paper says 9-12-87. The baby is due on grandma's birthday. I stare at the date, and then hand the paper to Chelsea. I look down at the bracelet Tessa gave me for Christmas. Grandma's sapphire birthstone dangles with mine. My baby will have that same birthstone. Tessa's going to flip out when I tell her.

****

"This is unfucking real," Chelsea says once we get back to Erica's car.

"What's unreal? What's going on?" Erica's looking from Chelsea to me.

"My baby's due on grandma's birthday," I say, smiling.

"Whoa, that's crazy," Erica says, holding her arms out to reveal goosebumps.

"Most babies aren't born on their actual due date," Chelsea says, pushing Erica's arms down so she can pretend that what's happening isn't amazing.

"Chelsea, come on! You have to know this is a sign." We haven't started driving yet. Erica knows this is a moment that requires our full attention.

Chelsea looks out the window. "I can't believe this."

"Me either," I say.

"Are you saying you want to have the baby?" Erica asks me.

"I want to have, and keep, the baby." I look at Chelsea.

She leans forward and buries her face in her hands. She's crying now. "This is going to ruin everything for you. How will you ever manage this? I get it now, okay? I heard the heartbeat, and I know this is real, but how will you do this?" Her shoulders bob up and down with every sentence and sob.

"I don't know," I say.

"How will you tell dad?" Chelsea asks me, wiping her eyes over and over again with her palms.

"I don't know that either."

All I know is that my life's going to be a mess from here on out.

****

Sitting at the kitchen table every night doing my homework while dad buzzes around the house clueless that I'm about to ruin his life is getting to be unbearable. At least my schoolwork seems like no big deal now that I have so many other things to worry about. Thankfully school comes easy to me because right now half my brain is being sucked up by the predicament I'm in.

I call Janet to check on Tessa. She said after Tessa read my note the other day, she saw a glimmer of a smile out of her. I know it was that part about worst week ever. To be honest, if Tessa knew the week I had, she would let me win. At some point, I'm going to show up at her house and blurt it out and pray to God that she doesn't tell me to leave. If she knows I am pregnant she will have something else to concentrate on—other than guilt. Or her guilt will be worse because I don't have Jason here with me. Oh God this situation is a giant heap of shit.

The due date means I'm now two months along, and the last day I was with Jason is, indeed, the day I got pregnant. Remembering back to cuddling in Jason's room all day brings a wave of so many different emotions over me. How did I get here? Sixteen and having a baby with a guy who is no longer on this Earth.

Chelsea and I spend most nights in her room after dad and Zachary have gone to bed brainstorming how to tell dad. We go back and forth about waiting until I'm farther along. I'm worried if we don't tell him now, he'll be even madder by the time I do.

"I've thought about this and thought about this, and if it were me, I think I'd write him a note and leave it for him to find," Chelsea says with so much gloom that her sadness settles in my chest like a bad winter cold.

"I had that same thought," I agree.

"I think you write the note tonight and then leave it in his room before we go to school. Tomorrow after he gets home from work, you'll have to deal with him, but at least you can get out what you need to say before he kills you." She stands and opens the drawer of her night stand. "You might as well get started. We can't keep on like this. He has to know." She hands me a pad of paper and pen.

"Where do I even start?"

"Start with the truth. Just tell him what happened."

I nod and stand to go up to my room.

"Come back down when you're done. I can read it over for you."

I nod again—this is really going to happen.

I go in my room and lay on my bedroom floor with my legs kicked behind me and just start writing.

*Dad,*

*I'm writing this letter so you have time to think about what I have to tell you. As you know by now, I had a boyfriend, and his name was Jason. He died in the accident. I loved him very much. I realize this makes you mad because I lied and went behind your back to be with him, but that's over now and I'm sorry.*

*Before I tell you my next thing, I want you to know we were responsible with our relationship. I was taking birth control pills, and he was a good guy. He loved me. Despite our efforts to be smart about sex, we failed. I recently found out that my strep throat meds canceled out my birth control. So, yes, it means what you think it does. I'm pregnant, Dad. I'm due on grandma's birthday.*

*This will come as a shock, but I feel like this baby's already part of our family. The baby is a Shine. I want to keep my baby, and I want to keep what remains of Jason. Don't worry about school. I plan to continue with school, doing a homebound program they offer pregnant teens. I can do this. I just need your support.*

*Now you know. I'm sorry this happened.*

*Love, Meg.*

I fold the letter and go back to Chelsea's room. Hands shaking, I toss it on her bed.

She snatches it up immediately. She reads

through it with lightning speed. "The school has a homebound program?" she asks.

"Yeah. I found out about it this week. What do you think about everything I said?"

"I think it's all you can say, adding the part about grandma and the due date might help your case, but I doubt it." She tosses the note back to me.

\*\*\*\*

The next day I drift through every one of my classes in a state of panic, worry, and dread until school is finally over. I kept waiting for my name to be called over the loud speaker signaling that dad had come to drag me home and lock me in my room forever. He could be home now waiting for me. I picture him sitting at the table with the note in his hand and his face on fire with anger. Packing up to leave the school with Chelsea and Erica, I'm stressed for what's about to happen. I want to run away and never look back, but that's stupid and I have nowhere to go.

"Whew, his Bronco's gone. He must still be at work," Chelsea says as Erica rounds the corner onto our street.

She was afraid he was home waiting like I thought he would be. This gives us time to settle in before I face my doom.

"Hurry up. Let's get inside before he pulls up from work early, and I'm just standing here. I don't want to see him." I rush to get out of the car.

"You have to see him some time. It's not like he's going to be gone all night," Erica says.

I ignore her and run into the house with Chelsea close behind. The minute we walk in the kitchen we both see the note I left him this morning sitting on the table— it's open.

"He read it." I start pacing as the nanny packs up

her things, turning Zach over to us.

Chelsea picks the note up and examines it for a second. "He wrote on it," she says, flipping the note over.

"What?" I stop pacing and look at her.

"Yeah, it only has one sentence written on it."

"What does it say?

"It says, I can't believe you've done this." She's silent, waiting for me to say something.

"That's it?"

She nods, handing me the note.

"What does that mean?" I'm so confused.

"I think it means what it says. It's pretty self-explanatory."

"What should I do right now?" I'm unsure of what to do with myself, and Zachery is staring at me. He can tell something is wrong.

Chelsea's looking at me without a response.

"Maybe I should be in my room when he gets home. Let him come to me if he wants, so I don't have to try talking to him the minute he walks in."

"Damn, that leaves me out here with Zach when he comes in," she says.

We are both terrified. I bolt to my room without another word.

\*\*\*\*

Three hours pass and still no dad. After finishing all my homework, cleaning out my sock drawer, and rearranging all the clothes in my closet, I wonder if he's even coming home. Maybe he ran away—I'd be fine with that. I'm just about to head to the bathroom when I hear the creak of the front door opening. I race to the window and see his Bronco on the driveway.

"Oh, shit, shit, shit." I race around my room in a circle like I'm trying to find shelter from a bomb about to

213

land on the house.

Should I go back to cleaning out my sock drawer to seem normal or should I crawl under my covers and hide like a five-year-old? Sitting down on my bed, I stare at the door, watching to see if a shadow appears under it, indicating that he's there.

He comes down the hall, wasting no time storming in my room. His curly hair has not been cut in a while, and he sort of has a mad clown look going on with it poofing out past his ears. "I guess you think you can lie to me, sneak around behind my back, and expect that I'm going to take care of your mistake?"

I want to yell, "It's not a mistake. It was an accident," but I think I should keep my thoughts to myself right now. I'm staring down at my bed, swishing a loose thread on my bedspread between my fingers.

"You by God better answer me." He's still standing at the door—but yelling now.

"No," I mutter.

"Are you in some sort of dreamland, Megan? You're sixteen, you don't make your own money, and you live off me. Your job right now is to live here and go to school. That doesn't include raising a kid with a guy who's not even here to help you."

I don't respond—I know he needs to get this out. And what would I say anyway? I hate that he's acting like Jason has a choice to be here or not.

"I'll tell you what my job doesn't entail, and that's helping you ruin your life by having a kid at sixteen."

I know he wants a response, but all I can do is look at him. I can see tears in his eyes that he refuses to let fall.

"You will have zero help from me. Do you hear me? Zero help."

My brother begins crying from the kitchen. Zachary hates when Dad yells.

"Do you understand me?" He bellows at me a second time and I flinch.

"Yes." I'm afraid to say anything else.

"No money, no babysitting, no baby supplies, and no pretending that this is okay."

I lower my eyes back to my bed and he walks away, leaving the door open like he did when I was little and he just gave me a spanking.

## Chapter Twenty-Four

My dad acts like I don't exist when I'm in the kitchen making toast for Zachary before school. Walking all the way around the table to avoid having to move past me, he won't even look at me. He talks to both Chelsea and my brother but does not acknowledge my presence in the room. It's weird, but it's better than yelling.

Zachary hasn't picked up on it, but it's making Chelsea fidgety and uncomfortable. I guess this is how he's going to handle his pregnant daughter—pretend there is no pregnant daughter. I want to tell him to grow up, but he would act like he didn't hear me.

"Chelsea, I'm off to work. The nanny should be here for Zachary at any minute." He leans down to look at Zachary. "Bye, buddy, have a good day. Bye, Chels." He doesn't even give a second glance toward me.

"Wow, what a dick," I say.

"Dick," Zachary says.

"Yep, that's right, buddy. That's exactly what he is."

At the school payphone, the same stupid girl is hogging the phone. For God's sake is this chick ever in class? I take the phone out of her hand mid-sentence and hang it up.

"Hey, what the hell?" She whines in a high-pitched squeal.

"Go ahead. I dare you to give me one ounce of shit today." I'm in no mood for her crap, and she knows it.

She stomps off as I fish two fingers through my jeans pocket to find some change to call Tessa. The phone rings like twenty times before I give up. That's it, I'm going to her house today. I can't do this without her for one more day.

\*\*\*\*

Lonnie's in the yard when Erica drops me at Tessa's. Winter is almost over, and he's dying to get his grass going again. He smiles at me as I go in the front door.

When I step in, I'm engulfed in the aroma of something wonderful. It smells like Janet pulled a casserole out of the oven, and my stomach growls. Tessa's house makes me feel calmer almost instantly. This fragrant, homey scent should be bottled up so kids with a less than stellar home life can open it and take a whiff from time to time. They could call it *The Home You Really Want*.

"Oh, Megan, honey, I didn't know you were coming over," Janet says, looking surprised but happy to see me.

"I haven't heard from Tess since the hospital, and I think it's time I push myself on her."

"I agree. She's not going to get better unless we force it on her." Janet looks up the stairs toward Tessa's room. "Good luck."

Tessa's hanging out the window smoking a cigarette when I go into her room.

"You know your dad's out front on the lawn." I startle her. "You're pretty ballsy not locking your door with a smoke in your hand."

She turns to look at me fully. Her face is still pink with the freshness of her last surgery, but it's looking slightly better. She still hasn't said a word to me. She takes the last puff off her cigarette and flicks it out the window.

"Well, I just came to tell you I win worst week ever. I'm pregnant, and my dad's basically pretending I'm dead now, so top that shit." I don't waste any time, and I'm hoping to hell I get some sort of reaction out of her with my huge confession.

She looks at me, stunned. *"Fuck a duck!"* She comes over to me faster than I've seen her move since the accident. She lifts my shirt and checks out my belly. "Are you kidding me? Is this some sort of, like, pull Tessa out of her misery stunt?" She's still looking at my bare stomach.

I pull my shirt down, shooing her hand away, and say, "I wish to hell it was, because I'm fucked in the fuckiest way possible."

"The fuckiest way possible?" This sends her into a fit of laughter and of course makes me laugh too. "This is, like, totally off the charts crazy," she says, calming down and looking at me seriously now. "I'm sorry, Meg. I've been a total asshole. I'm kind of a mess."

"You don't owe me an explanation, Tess. It's okay. You've been through a lot."

"I've been trying to forget," she says.

"Forget what?" I sit on her bed, hoping she'll come sit down and explain it all to me.

"Trying to forget days. Like I just want to forget the last two months. I can't handle thinking about Riley and Jason." She looks at me. "And you. It hurts too much."

When she says this, I know it's time for me to let her know that I don't blame her for the accident. "Yeah, you're trying to forget because life's been a real bitch for you, and I want you to know none of that's your fault. It's not anyone's fault. Grandma always told me that life will throw you heartbreak at every stage without any fault of your own, but heartbreak means you truly loved someone or something and that's a gift that we should never forget. You're going to get better and we're going to do it together. Are you listening to me? Stop blaming yourself because I don't and neither would Jason or

Riley."

She smiles a tiny smile, and I can see how badly she needs to find the truth in my words. That car wreck broke more than Tessa's face and arm—it broke her spirit.

"I can't believe you're going to have a baby." She knows me well enough to know that I'm having the baby.

"It's due on grandma's birthday."

The minute I say it, she looks at me stunned again. "Jason's baby due on your grandma's birthday. I'm starting to believe that life's nothing but an emotional rollercoaster and you only get off when you die."

I lean in to give her a hug.

"Megan Shine giving hugs. This must be another miracle."

"Shut it," I say but squeeze her harder, realizing she just referred to my baby as a miracle.

"You're like the bravest person I know. Telling your dad had to have been the scariest shit you've ever done," she says.

"I don't know about brave. I'm scared to death."

"And, yet, you're choosing the baby. That's bravery in my book."

"Well, some would call it stupidity. So, I'll take bravery."

\*\*\*\*

I'm devouring pizza and watching Pretty in Pink at Tessa's, and it feels good to be back to normal … well, our new normal. We don't sit around sipping schnapps or sneak out to parties anymore, and I've even been able to talk her out of smoking cigarettes most days. I've spent most of my non-babysitting time here over the last month. Dad could care less where I am. I guess since I'm already pregnant he figures I can't get into any more trouble than I'm already in. Janet knows I'm pregnant by now. She's so thrilled I'm here, and Tessa seems back to her old self, that she doesn't care what's going on as long as Tessa's happy.

"That was like the best Molly Ringwald yet," Tessa says as we lounge on her bed, and I think about eating more of the leftover pizza. My appetite has really picked up lately, especially now that I don't feel like puking all the time anymore.

"I don't know, I think I still vote Sixteen Candles," I say.

"Yeah, but Sixteen Candles doesn't have Ducky, and you can't discount the duck man."

"This is true," I agree. I run my hand over my belly, and for the first time, I feel it's safe to wonder if I'm having a boy or a girl. I look at Tessa and say, "Boy or girl?"

Without even hesitating, Tessa says, "Girl."

"Really? I'm thinking boy."

"Boy? No way. We need a girl baby so she can be totally bitchin like her Aunt Tessa. Which do you want?" Tessa asks curiously.

"Well, I'd love to have a boy that looks like Jason. Plus, I do know about little boys thanks to Zachary. It would be cool to have a girl, too. All the fun clothes and hair stuff you can do with girls would be exciting. I guess I'll be happy with either," I say.

Even talking about this seems so unreal, but I'm getting used to the idea.

"So, tell me, like, what are the names swirling around in that head of yours?" Tessa says as I start painting her nails. Tessa's enjoying the pampering. She looks relaxed leaning against her headboard with her eyes closed.

"If it's a boy, I'll name him Jason without a

doubt."

"Of course," she says.

"I have no clue what I'd name a girl. Absolutely no idea." I think and think, and I can't come up with one name I would consider for something so important. "What do you want to name your daughter someday?"

"I'm not having kids. They're all a big pain in the ass," Tessa says.

"Tessa!" I shout at her.

She opens her good eye slightly and peeps at me before shutting it again. "Fine your kid won't be a pain in the ass, but I'm terrified I'd, like, have a kid exactly like me, and I know I'm a total pain in the ass." *At least Tessa knows she's a pain in the ass*, I think.

\*\*\*\*

Since my pregnant belly's out for the world to see now, everyone at school stares at me like I grew an extra limb.

"You going to eat the rest of your lunch?" I ask Chelsea as I sit next to her in the school cafeteria.

"No, go ahead. You need it more than I do." She scoots her tray toward me.

I'm surprised she sits with me during lunch now.

Looking down at my clothes, I say, "How long do you think I can keep wearing this shirt? It's barely covering the top of my jeans."

She looks at my shirt. "Well, at the rate you're growing, not much longer. Maybe you could sneak and wear some of dad's shirts," she says.

My jeans no longer button, so I have to leave them undone with a rubber band around the buttons to make more room. I keep wondering if dad will buy me maternity clothes—but he's not offering.

"Oh, yeah right, I already look like a weirdo. Adding men's clothes to my wardrobe will make it so

221

much better." I stuff the roll off her tray in my mouth.

"I'll call Bertie. She might have something for you to wear."

"Old lady clothes, I think I'll pass."

"Well you can't keep on wearing your clothes. You look like you're wearing Zach's shirt."

This makes me laugh because I see her point. "Well, I guess Bertie's clothes couldn't make them gawk at me any worse," I say, looking over at a table full of kids whispering about me. They don't even look away when I glare back.

Chelsea tells me to ignore all the stares and reminds me that none of the kids we go to school with would have the balls to do what I'm doing. Chelsea gets more upset about the rudeness from other people than I do. I know my grades are still better than half these judgmental assholes, so I ignore them. She's team baby now and furious at the way I'm being treated.

The baby kicks and tiny flutters hum in my belly. I think about Jason every time I feel the tiny pinging. Sometimes I want to call Kenny or his mom and tell them about the baby, but I know better. They are drug addicts and I've known that since I met them. I can't and won't raise my baby around that life.

It's sad because they don't realize a part of Jason is still here on this Earth swimming around in my body. They are too high to realize anything to be honest. Maybe someday they will be different, but for now I'm protecting my baby from them. I don't care if it's selfish—it's not about me anymore.

## Chapter Twenty-Five

"You totally pumped for your ultrasonic?" Tessa's procrastinating instead of doing her homework that'll finish out her classes for the school year. She's busy interrupting my study time. I have my last two finals tomorrow at school, and she's making it impossible to concentrate.

"It's called an ultrasound, you weirdo."

"Like, same thing."

"And to answer your question, yes, I'm completely stoked to see the baby."

"Forget about seeing it, I only want to know if it's a boy or a girl."

"Tessa!"

"Fine. I want to, like, see its little body or whatever."

"Stop talking, and get your damn homework done. We're almost free for the summer." I can't believe I won't be going back to high school ever again. This homebound school thing is going to be bizarre. My dad had to sign off on the homebound paperwork and he refused. I left it on his dresser for a whole week before I gave up and forged his signature. He wasn't kidding when he said I'll have zero help from him. The baby isn't even here yet and he's being a stubborn ass.

\*\*\*\*

The day of the ultrasound Janet drives me, Tessa, and Chelsea to the hospital. She's very upset with the way my dad is handling my pregnancy and wanted to at least be there for me when we find out the sex of the baby. We're all worked up with excitement when the nurse calls me back. It feels good to be excited about something for once even if I'm scared shitless.

We crowd in around the little monitor, and I'm

speechless as I watch my baby move around inside me. It's amazing how I can see the outline of the spine and hands. There isn't a dry eye in the room when the nurse asks me if I want to know the sex of the baby. We all say, "Yes" at the same time, and she laughs.

"Okay, Megan, you're having a baby girl."

Tessa high-fives Chelsea and Janet wipes her eyes. Janet's sad I don't have my parents here.

"I knew we'd get a girl," Tessa says, genuinely thrilled about that fact.

I'm having a daughter—Jason's little girl. The hole in my heart that formed by the loss of Jason is filled back up when his daughter moves around on the screen in front of me.

"That's it. We're totally going shopping. I've been saving my allowance, and we're going to, like, go buy this baby every purple item of clothing we can totally find," Tessa says.

"Tess, you called it. Maybe you thought I needed a break from little boys for a change."

"You totally better pray like hell she won't be anything like us." Tessa points to my belly and laughs at the thought of that.

"Hey, I think if she's anything like us she'll be lucky. We are some tough chicks. Although, I'm banning her from boys," I say. As soon as I say it, I understand my dad's struggle raising daughters.

All of a sudden, I get why he didn't want us around boys. How funny that I never understood him until I did the very thing he was afraid of. I'm not saying I agree with the way he has shut me out, but I get why he's so over the top with the rules. Too bad I can't tell him this—he ignores everything I say.

"Yes, you are very tough young ladies. I'm proud of all of you. This has been a tough year and you've all persevered." Janet gives Tessa a side hug.

Tears continue down my face, but they're no longer tears of sorrow. I'm going to figure this out for me and for my daughter. For now, all I can do is pray like hell that when the baby comes I've figured out how.

****

Even though I'm pregnant and my feet are swollen to the size of Chicago—I'm having the best summer of my life. Every day Tessa and I go to the pool with Chelsea and Erica. Tessa has to wear a giant hat to keep the sun off her face since the skin's so delicate after her last surgery.

They never get over cracking up at me in my bathing suit. Bertie bought me a bathing suit meant for older pregnant women, and I look like a giant blueberry because it's a dark-blue one-piece that emphasizes my round belly.

Zachary rubs my round belly and says, "Baby in there, Gan." There's no way to explain any of this to a toddler, but he knows a baby is coming.

Chelsea finds it hysterical that Zachary is going to be an uncle when he isn't even three yet. She calls him Uncle Zachary and doubles over with laughter.

The closer I get to my due date, the more pressure there is to come up with her name. I can't decide. Everyone has come up with names for me, of course, and I love some of them—well not Tessa's. She thinks I should name her Joan Jett. I agree Joan Jett is a bad ass, but I'm not naming my daughter after her. This is going to be her name. She'll have this name forever, and I can't take the pressure. I tell Chelsea that I should wait until I see her and then name her.

"You can't treat her like a dog. You name a dog when you meet them, not a baby." Chelsea says I have to have a name for her before she's here, but I don't know why it's such a big deal.

"Says who?" I ask her.

"Says everyone. Pick a damn name already."

It's funny because I think it truly makes her anxious that I don't have a name yet. I know she's a little afraid I will name the baby after Tessa, but I'm not doing that either. There can only be one Tessa in my life, and she is plenty.

On top of the name issue, I'm terrified of labor. Chelsea checked out labor videos for me at the library. Instead of helping to prepare me—they scared the hell out of me. She sat on the couch with me and went over the breathing, but I only giggled because Tessa tried practicing the breathing too.

The hospital agreed to let me have Janet, Tessa, and Chelsea in my delivery room. I could tell on our visit to the hospital that this annoyed them, but I need them all with me. Of course, Chelsea and Tessa might be in class at school, but Janet said we should put everyone on the list in case it happened on a weekend. Tessa made Janet promise to get her out of school if it happened during the school day.

****

I try not to get depressed when I go school-clothes shopping with Chelsea and Tessa the next weekend. Erica drove us all to the mall, and I waddle behind them as they go from store to store. Chelsea's getting excited for school to start so she can wear the new outfits she's buying.

"I think I need to go sit in the food court while you guys finish up." I've been shopping with them for two hours and my feet and back are throbbing. It's Labor Day weekend and the mall is packed with people wanting to catch a sale.

"Do you feel okay?" Chelsea looks at me,

frowning with concern.

"I feel like a beached whale, and I'm getting hungry anyway. I think I'll go sit at Orange Julius and have a smoothie."

"I don't think we have too much longer. I want to stop at one more store and I'll be done," Tessa says.

Chelsea and Erica nod.

"Take all the time you want, because once I sit down, I'm not going to want to get back up for a bit."

"You're sure you're okay?" Chelsea says again.

"Yes, yes. I'm fine." I wave them away.

"Okay, if you're sure. We'll be back in less than an hour," Chelsea says.

The closer I get to my due date—grandma's birthday—the more Chelsea gets anxious about leaving me alone. She told me that Erica told her that some women die in childbirth. Tessa told her that Erica's a dumbass. Why would Erica even say something like that? Leave it to Erica to cause us all to have that in the back of our minds now. Janet says that never happens anymore. If it does, it usually only happens when something was wrong before delivery or someone who is not trained in the first place tries to deliver the baby at home.

By the time I get downstairs to the food court, queasiness has started to set in. I go ahead and buy the smoothie, but halfway through it, I'm wondering if I might puke. I've totally overdone it today. Too much walking, and the heat outside has not helped my swollen ankles at all.

I watch as everyone bustles by with bags of clothes, and I think about how this would've been me if not for strep throat. It's insane how life works out. Who knew that a strep throat infection could turn out like this? Last year on this same weekend, I was here arguing with

Chelsea about how much money we each got from the clothes allowance Dad gave us. She argued that she should get more because she's older. I remember telling her that she was the dumbest person alive to think that's fair. I laugh to myself at how petty we were to each other just a year ago.

The baby has changed us for the better—and she isn't even here yet. The baby has brought me closer to everyone in my life except Dad. I'd give anything to tell Jason all about how the last nine months have gone for me. He would hate my dad for this, and I wouldn't blame him. Although I don't hate Dad, I feel sorry for him. He lost a wife, mother, daughter, and now granddaughter— and still found a way to keep up his stubborn attitude. All I can do is pray for change. Grandma would say, "Meggie, all you can do is pray for change and keep lovin." I can see her smoking a cigarette at the kitchen table and talking to Bertie on the phone. I miss her more with every passing day, but the pain of that longing has faded.

I'm debating going to the bathroom when they all walk toward me. "Perfect timing. That smoothie isn't setting well in my stomach, and I want to get home."

"Your stomach has felt like shit all day. You need to drink some water. My mom told you to be drinking it all day, remember? Have you had any since we got here?" Now Tessa's starting in on me with her worry.

"I drank, like, a gallon of water today. I need to go home and rest, I think."

Chelsea and Tessa help me up while Erica gathers all the bags. As I stand up, a gush of water comes out of me. I even feel some sort of internal pop like a champagne cork blasting away from the bottle.

"Oh shit," I say and look at the liquid puddling at my feet.

"What the hell's that?" Chelsea takes a step back.

"Her water broke. We have to get her to the hospital now," Tessa starts shouting at us, even though we're all standing right next to her.

All at once, they start dragging me toward the front doors of the mall, trying to carry their bags at the same time. Tessa's hollering for people to get the hell out of our way. I need a towel between my legs. I didn't realize when my water broke there would be this much fluid. I'm sure we look crazy—three teenage girls, loaded down with shopping bags, rushing a pregnant girl through the mall while she leaves a path of liquid.

"Erica, run ahead and get the car pulled up," Tessa directs her.

"Good thinking," Erica says and shoots toward the doors.

It seems like it takes forever to get to the parking lot, but when we do, Erica's waiting for us. She jumps out and throws all the bags into her trunk, and Chelsea and Tessa climb in back.

"Oh my God. I'm sorry about your seats," I say to Erica as I ease my wet butt onto the front seat.

"Who cares about the seats? The only person that ever sits there is your sister. It's time to have us a baby." She looks over and smiles at me.

A pain slams into my back. "Oh shit! Hurry up," I say. "She's coming!"

## Chapter Twenty-Six

We pull up to the Emergency Room drop-off and Erica slams on the breaks so sudden it's like she's breaking for an animal in the middle of the road or something. It throws all of us forward.

"Shit, sorry," she says to us.

"Oh God, this is the wrong place," I pant. "I'm to go to the Labor and Delivery drop-off."

"Oh Jesus, sorry." She punches the gas pedal, giving us all whiplash again.

I can tell she's flustered, because my labor pains have gotten worse, and I'm doubled over in her car.

"Right, I knew that, dammit."

Tessa's rubbing my shoulders from behind and Chelsea's crying. I knew Chelsea would bring out the dramatics. All the fear and anxiety she has had over the last month are now coming to head with me in labor. What will she do when she has her own kids someday?

"Chelsea, I'm going to be fine, so knock off the crying, would ya?" I say in between moans.

"I'm scared, okay?" she says, blubbering from the backseat.

"Why the hell are you scared? I'm the one who has to push a human being out today. Plus, we're at a hospital, you know with doctors in it?" I'm laughing at her now, and then another wave of pain hits me. "Oh, dear God, this hurts."

The car skids to a stop, and Erica flies out of the driver's seat when we get to the Labor and Delivery curb. She runs inside. I'm not sure why she leaves me behind, but then she comes running out with a wheelchair.

"Good idea," I say as Tessa pulls me out of the car carefully by both my hands. I sit down in the wheelchair as another pain knocks the breath out of me it's so strong. It feels like someone has stuck a knife in my lower back and they've decided to twist it. "Holy fuck," I shout, and Erica hurriedly wheels me inside.

Chelsea's still crying and running alongside us.

The front desk lady moves around to us when she sees me coming. "How far apart are the contractions?" she asks us.

"Um, Meg?" Tessa looks at me.

"How the hell do I know? My water broke over a half hour ago!"

"Oh dear. You're sure your water broke?" she says to me.

"Lady, I created a puddle the size of a pond at the mall and if you don't mind, I'd like to get to a hospital room before … oh Jesus … this baby comes." I'm getting pissed now as the pain is worsening.

Tessa goes to the phone at the hospital desk to call Janet, and Chelsea worthlessly continues blubbering to herself.

The lady goes over to her desk and makes a call while keeping her eyes on me.

The pains are hitting me faster now, and I scream out in agony.

Chelsea tries to hug me, and I scream at her to get off. She's now hugging herself and rocking back and forth. She looks like she has escaped from the psych ward the way she's mumbling to herself.

Tessa's giving the lady at reception my name and information.

When I look up, I see two nurses coming my way. They wheel me back to a room giving Erica and Chelsea instructions on how to help me get a gown on while they prep something behind me.

The pain is unbearable, and I don't even remember getting in the gown when Tessa comes in to tell me that Janet's on her way. Tessa wants an adult here that isn't a stranger.

I'm curled in a ball with sweat pouring down my face, and it's like I'm being stabbed in the back and punched in my stomach at the same time. It's a rolling pain that shoots through me every ten seconds or so. I can barely catch my breath when the next pain comes.

"Something's wrong," I pant.

The blonde nurse who has a perky ponytail on top of her head and God-awful blue eyeshadow tells me that this is how labor goes.

"What are you feeling right now?" The other nurse, who has a brown, bob haircut and glasses is standing beside me now, too.

"There's heaviness down there," I say, rolling around in the bed, trying to get away from the pain.

"Well, this is your first baby, and it can be hard to tell what normal pain feels like with your first one."

The ponytail nurse gets my legs up in stirrups and tells me she's going to check to see how far I've dilated. A moment later, she says, "Oh wow. Get Dr. Thompson now!"

The brown-haired nurse hurries out of the room, and the other nurse looks at Erica, Tessa, and Chelsea.

"Okay, girls, I can see the top of the baby's head. If you can't handle this, I want you to go to the waiting room immediately."

Chelsea begins hyperventilating and wringing her hands.

"Also, we don't need you stressing the mother out. Either stop all that crying, or go sit down." The nurse is getting serious now. She knows that she's dealing with a bunch of teenagers, and she's probably wondering where the hell my mother is.

"What can we do?" Tessa asks.

"I want one of you on each side of her, holding her hands. She's going to have to start pushing."

At this point, we're all ignoring Chelsea. She thinks I'm dying, and nobody has time to calm her down—I think I actually might be dying.

"Hi, Megan. I'm Dr. Thompson." A tall man with dark hair comes to the top of the bed. "It looks like it's time to have a baby."

I'm want to yell, "No shit, can you get down there and do your job? Stop with all the 'hello' and 'blah, blah, blah!'"

He sits in a chair perched between my legs like he's getting ready to watch a Broadway play. "Now, when I tell you to push, I want you to push with all you've got until I say stop. Got it?" He peers around at me.

"Got it," I puff.

"Okay, Megan. Push."

I grip Tessa and Erica's hands and push as hard as I can until a burning down there stops me.

"Megan. I did not say stop. Now, push." The doctor is talking forcefully but somehow calmly as well.

"It hurts too much," I wheeze.

"You can do this, Meg," Tessa says to me. "Now, push!"

I push until I have nothing left, and the doctor tells me to take a rest. Chelsea's by my side now and looks like she might pass out.

"Okay, Megan. Get ready to push when I say go," Dr. Thompson says.

I take a deep breath in like I need all the air in the room to have the strength for this next push.

"Okay go," Dr. Thompson says.

I hold all that air in and all at once I let it out in a whoosh, pushing so hard I feel my girl parts rip apart.

The doctor instructs Tessa to hold my shoulders up from behind because I'm too exhausted now to push and hold myself up at the same time. I'm afraid I have nothing left, but I summon the strength to give it one more try and push like my life depends on it because it probably does. I finally feel her head out, and I'm so relieved to have accomplished that much. This gives me the motivation I need to get her all the way out. Pushing so hard that I'm screaming, I feel her slide the rest of the way out of my body. It is the weirdest sensation I've ever felt. The girls are all excited and crying when I look down to see the doctor place a little baby with a full head of dark, golden, wet hair on my chest.

"You have a beautiful baby girl, Megan," Dr. Thompson says. "What's her name?"

I lay back and take one look at her and say, "Loretta Valentine Shine."

I didn't know I would name her after grandma until that moment. Valentine as her middle name came out of my mouth, too. Jason loved my quirky middle name so I think he would've suggested it if he were here. She has his nose and mouth, and I kiss her little heart-shaped lips and cry and cry. Jason comes back to me from within her. I never knew you could love something as deeply as I love her. It's like a love that swallows my heart but in a good way.

"That's a lovely name," Dr. Thompson says.

We're all silent with amazement at how tiny and perfect she is. They take her, weigh her, and clean her up. By the time Janet comes in, I'm no longer in stirrups.

"I can't believe how fast you delivered her. I heard you did a great job," Janet says.

Janet and Chelsea are standing over Loretta watching the nurse swaddle her in a pink newborn blanket. They're smiling and hugging each other. I think we all know this baby's part of all of our families now.

Janet laughs when she looks at us.

"Hey! What's so funny?" Erica says.

"Well, you all look exhausted, not just Megan."

The girls look at each other and crack up.

"That was a lot of work," Chelsea says and we laugh even harder as she wipes sweat from her forehead.

After an hour of me trying to breastfeed, they all go to get some dinner in the cafeteria while I continue trying to get Loretta to latch on, the way the nurse showed me.

As she looks at me with her grayish-blue eyes, I whisper to her that I'm new to breastfeeding, so she needs to bear with me. I tell her that she'll need to bear with me on most things, but that I'll take care of her the best I can, and I love her.

She falls asleep, and I decide to close my eyes for a minute. I'm wore out. It's not easy pushing an eight-pound baby out of your body. I can't believe she weighs eight pounds. Grandma would've called her a whopper.

With my eyes closed, Zachary's voice floats into my room. Is that Zachary, or am I too tired to tell if that's some other kid? I look at the doorway leading out to the hall in time to see Zachary scurry by, followed by my dad chasing him.

"Zachary. Gan isn't down that way, come back," dad says.

I look down at Loretta and back up at the doorway. I'm shocked that dad came.

Zachary comes barreling back toward my end of the hall. My dad catches his arm right before he shoots past my room again.

When dad walks in, I try to sit up a bit more. It's like I'm afraid I'm in trouble.

He struggles to make eye contact with me for a

moment. I'm not sure if he's waiting for me to say something.

"Chelsea called. She ... well, she said you had the baby."

"I did." It's obvious because I'm holding a baby, but I don't know what he wants me to say. He hasn't spoken to me in so long that it's like we've forgotten how to talk to one another.

He walks closer to my bed and peers over at her.

"Meet Loretta Valentine Shine," I say, turning her so he can see her better.

With fat tears streaming down his face, he puts his hands out for her while Zachary bats at the balloon he's holding.

I tighten the blanket around her better and whisper into her ear, "It's time to say hello to your Grandpa Shine and Uncle Zachary."

As I hand her over, I look at Zachary. Chelsea's right, saying Uncle Zachary is hilarious.

I can see in dad's eyes that he's already in love with Loretta. Jason and Grandma are with me right now. The memories of love they left behind swirl around the room like invisible spirits. I've never felt so much peace in all my life. Grandma was right about fighting for love. I fought for Loretta and in the end, we won—we're going to be okay.

"Will you call her Loretta?" Dad asks, holding her face up to his.

"I was thinking about calling her Sunshine."

## The End

**Evernight Teen ®**

**<ins>www.evernightteen.com</ins>**

Made in the USA
Monee, IL
07 September 2020

41585370R00142